SCAMMERS

AN ILLUMINATI NOVEL

SLMN

Kingston Imperial

Scammers Copyright © 2021 by Kingston Imperial 2, LLC

Printed in the United States of America

Rights Department, 144 North 7th Street, #255 Brooklyn N.Y. 11249

First Edition:

Book and Jacket Design: Damion Scott & PixiLL Designs

Cataloging in Publication data is on file with the library of Congress

ISBN 9781733304139

PROLOGUE

The bike's engine roared into life. The rider twisted the throttle grip twice. The roar became a threatening growl. A heartbeat later a woman came running towards him. She threw one leg over the machine, straddling it, and wrapped one arm around him. She gave him a thumbs up over his shoulder. He released the clutch.

She could feel the power of the machine between her legs. The engine throbbed. The sheer power of the machine raced through her body. It had been a while since she'd last ridden, but the thrill of it was seared into her. In so many ways it was better than sex.

She'd always been happy to ride on the back of a bike, confident enough in her balance not to hang onto whoever had control of the machine, but today she wanted to be close to him. To *feel* him.

They were getting out of there before any more shit went down.

They were getting out of town with their lives and a big old bag of cash; she needed him to know she was happy about what was happening. Scratch that. *More* than happy.

"Are you nervous?" Myers said and leaned back in his chair, the soft light of the courtroom bulbs glinting off his glasses.

He laid his pen down on the pad in front of him, folding his arms across his chest and waited.

It wasn't the first time Jordan had been questioned in the dock, but this time it felt different. Even so, she was reluctant to talk, despite the fact she'd sworn to, so help her God.

She wasn't sure *why*.

She glanced at the female court official leaning against the wall behind him. She had her arms folded against her chest, clearly bored and wishing she was anywhere else than there. She wasn't there because anyone thought Jordan was dangerous, and even if she was, she'd be a fool to try anything in Court Room I. It would be a death sentence.

"A little," she admitted, with a shrug. There didn't seem to be any point in lying to the DA about something as small as that. She didn't have anything to hide, so why should she lie? At least that was what she kept telling herself. She eyed the glass of water on the little shelf in front of her and almost reached out to take a sip, but that would look bad to the jury. That would look like she was trying to cover her nerves.

She just wanted this to be over with so she could stop second guessing herself.

It shouldn't have been so stressful, especially with Myers smiling reassuringly at her. That smile of his seemed genuine, but looks could be deceiving. But, maybe this was just routine after all, and she was spooking herself for nothing? It wasn't like there was much she could tell them. She couldn't remember shit she couldn't remember, even with her hand on the bible. And that meant she couldn't remember much of anything apart from her mother. So much had been taken away from her. Problem was, she had no idea what that shit might have been before it was gone.

"Don't be. Take a deep breath. We're all with you."

She did as she was told. She sucked in the air, tasted the stale and bitter lingering scent of sweat from all the guilty souls who'd been in the room before. She held that breath for a moment, then let it out slowly.

"You ready?" He asked without any sign of impatience. He was clearly used to this. To talking an unwilling or unsteady witness through their memories.

She looked at the judge. He nodded encouragingly.

She nodded to the DA. Time to get this over with. The sooner she was done, the sooner she could get out of there and back to whatever was left of her life.

"Great, okay...How about you tell us when you first met Minx?"

"Right—right after the accident," she replied. "I met her in the hospital."

"Good. That's great. And what do you remember about the accident?" He asked, not looking at the line of faces in the jury or anyone else. It was as if they were the only two people in the courtroom. The stenographer transcribed every word.

"Not much. I'm sorry. It all happened so quickly. I'm not even sure if what I *think* I can remember is just something I've put together from what people have told me, and things I've overheard."

"Don't be. The doctors say that it's common among patients with severe head trauma. More often than not they

3

won't remember everything that happened with any kind of clarity, and that's not just the event itself. I'm no expert, but they assure me that with most people, things start to come back with time. So, you'll just need to give it time." He said that like it was a good thing. "Now tell me about Minx," Myers said.

She sipped her water, then sifted back, past the lies, the betrayals, and the blood...so much blood. *Stay focused*, some part of her subconscious mind warned. She closed her eyes, gathered her thoughts, and began...

JORDAN

"What's your name?" the young woman asked.

Jordan didn't know why she was in her hospital room, but she was glad of the company. The fact that she wore a hospital gown, made her leap to the obvious conclusion that she was another patient. A fellow traveler through pain and misery.

Doctors and nurses had been coming and going for what seemed like days. None of them had found the time to stop and talk; not really talk. She wanted to know what had happened to her, but none of them were willing to offer her anything much beyond the fact that she'd been in a traffic accident. They kept checking in to ask how she was feeling, but it was all very clinical. They didn't want to hear that she was frightened, only if she felt nausea or other symptoms that might suggest they'd missed something. She'd heard whispers of a brain bleed, but had no clue if it was what she'd had or what they were afraid of. Still, any company was better than being alone.

"Jordan," she said. "What's yours?"

Jordan eased herself up in bed a little, but the movement hurt without making her more comfortable. She thought about trying to get out of bed and sitting in the chair for a while, but her body told it wasn't ready for that with a sharp stab of pain.

"Minx," the young woman replied with a smile that dimpled her check, and perched herself on the edge of the bed.

Interesting. She chose not to take the chair for herself.

Jordan mustered a smile of her own in return.

Minx reminded her of someone she knew, but couldn't place. Like the ghost of a memory trapped in the mists of her past. Maybe she was someone she knew? Or had known? Someone she'd met before?

But then would she have needed to ask her name?

Or was it some kind of test?

Her short pixie hair cut made her look tom-boyish and more than a little mischievous. She had the body to match that impishness. There was something sensual and alluring...even dangerous about her. Because none of it was innocent. Looking at her now Jordan figured the woman would have turned plenty of heads, including... there was a name there for a second, about to jump out from the fog, the name of someone she had known, maybe even someone was close to... But then it was gone.

She tried not to let the frustration get to her.

She's all the things I'm not, Jordan had thought with more than a little envy.

"The devil don't get this one," her mother would say to no one in particular, red hand raw after spanking Jordan. That was just the way it was in her household. Her mother, a pastor in Savannah, Georgia used to beat her for the slightest of reason, or no reason at all. Jordan wondered why this was the one memory that had stuck when damned near everything else had deserted her?

Was it significant?

Spare the rod and spoil the child was the code her mother lived by.

But her mother knew she'd had her work cut out with this particular child, like the devil was in her and he shone through her pretty face.

Shy didn't matter, she had a beauty that stood out.

Grown men had secretly lusted after her since she was twelve, and some of them not so secretly. She'd seen the way they had looked at her, even if she had been too innocent to know what those looks had meant at first. Her face was angelic, shining bright with that innocent purity men lusted after, oh so fucking desperate to defile. She'd been gorgeous even then, leaving childhood behind long before she was a teenager. It was a dangerous road for any girl to wander alone.

Jordan winced again as she shifted in the bed.

Her entire body was sore and bruised, joints and muscles thrown out of place and still trying to find their way back to a skeleton that made sense. It was a miracle, they assured her, that she was alive, so a few aches and pains were nothing.

"You okay?" Minx asked, shifting on the edge of the bed as her bony ass threatened to slip off the side.

"Yes," Jordan said, though it came out more as a wheeze than a word.

"There was an accident. At least that's what I heard the nurses say. Sounds like it was pretty bad. You were on the back of the bike, but I heard whoever was in front of you died."

Jordan stopped and looked at her.

"Died?"

"Yeah, I guess... that's what they sayin'. I'm sorry for your loss," she shrugged and Jordan wondered if she meant it. "Who was it?"

Jordan thought, trying to force her mind past the brick wall that had been built long before she even reached the hospital. Every brick was five inches thick and between them they hid *almost* everything that had happened in her life, including the identity of whoever had been on that bike with her.

"I don't... I mean I know it sounds stupid... but I don't know." Maybe it was whoever had almost popped into her head; the guy whose head would have been turned at the sight of Minx. She drifted away in thought, trying to force herself to remember and knowing that what she was doing really was just imagining what it was like on the back of that motorcycle.

The nurse knocked once on the glass door, then entered with an all-business smile on her lips. She didn't give Minx so much as a sideways glance. Minx slid off the bed to stand by the window, out of the way.

"How are you doing today, sugar?" The nurse asked as she picked up Jordan's chart from the bed of the bed. She wasn't listening to any reply. She read the chart.

"Sore," Jordan admitted, which was seriously underplaying it.

"You're blessed to be feeling anything young lady, you know that? God was smiling on you when this happened. Another inch and you'd have been looking at life in a wheel-chair. It was that close. Now, you tell me, how's your head today?"

"It throbs some when I lay on my side."

"Then you know the medicine you need for that? You don't lay on your side," the nurse laughed gently, adding, "Really, it's just the swelling. You can already see it's gone down some since you were brought in, but it still has a way to go." She produced a couple of pills in a small paper cup with deft slight of hand of a corner boy. "Here take these."

"One pill makes you smaller," Jordan said, washing the two tablets down with water.

"Just rest up, sugar. The doctor will be by to see you later," she made a note of something on the chart then slid it back into place, before turning for the door.

"Umm, nurse," Jordan called.

"Yes?"

"The person driving the bike... the one who died... what was their name?"

The nurse looked deeply uncomfortable with the question, then deflected it, "Why don't you wait until you talk to the doctor. When he gives the okay the police want to talk with you."

With that she walked out.

"Fucking bitch. She knows, you know she does, that look... She just don't want to say," Minx gruffed.

Jordan didn't respond.

She pushed her mind back into the darkness, but there was nothing inside the fog. She couldn't remember anyone other than her mother and this vague recollection of men who'd looked at her like meat when she was young.

I wish it had been her, Jordan thought, and instantly regretted it, not knowing why she should.

The pills began to take effect.

It wasn't long before she drifted into a deep drug-fueled sleep.

ALEXIS

"I can't believe you'd say *that* to me!" Alexis sobbed.

Devante stood over her, making her feel small.

"Bitch, you a stripper! I know goddamn well I ain't the only nigga you fuckin!" He spat, cold as ice, chest heaving, real anger only a heartbeat away from exploding.

She looked up at him with her baby blues, mascara running like black tears down her cheeks.

It wasn't a pretty sight.

"Is that all I am to you, Devante? A stripper? Really? Wasn't I there for you when you got hurt and you thought your career was over? Wasn't I? Did I ever judge *you*? No. Have I ever asked you for a dime? You gonna answer that honestly?"

Devante dropped his head and sighed; he knew she was right, about all of it.

"No."

"Then *why* you think I would lie to you now? I'm pregnant, Devante and it's yours. I may be a stripper, an exotic dancer, but you know that don't make me no whore!" Alexis shouted.

"I know…"

Even though they were alone in his hotel suite, a far cry from when they had first met, he still looked around, scared someone might overhear. Good scandal shit like this was worth money to those bottom feeders. His mind was spinning. "Look, ma, you don't have to yell. Okay? For real, TMZ has been known to buy rooms and shit," he said, full of paranoia. "Anything to get a story. And you and me... we a story."

Alexis stood up.

Even though his mind was all over the place, he couldn't deny her beauty. She was the baddest girl he'd ever laid eyes on. Just looking at her had his dick stiffening. Always did. She could always do that to him.

"You know what, Devante? Fuck you," she huffed, folding her arms across her chest. She'd been tempted to stamp her feet. He could see it in her eyes.

He grabbed her arm.

"Wait a minute. Don't leave, ma. You say you're pregnant. You sure?"

"Did I fuckin' stutter?"

"Then let's be sure, you know, get proof before we blow shit up," he replied with a sly smile.

"What, you a doctor or something? You want me to piss in your hand and see if it turn blue?"

He grabbed his phone.

"Naw, we can save the piss play for later, ma. I'm gonna get my man to pick up a pregnancy test," he told her, and before she could answer, he spoke into the phone. "Yo, you still in the room? I need you to do me a solid. Go get me one of them piss on a stick pregnancy tests."

"Make sure he get First Step cause they the most accurate," she chimed in, arms still folded across her chest, all set to be proved right.

"You hear the lady? Get one called First Step, okay? Yeah, and hurry the fuck up, too." Devante killed the call. He looked at her and took a breath. "So, if you *are* pregnant, and I ain't callin' you a liar, ma... just saying when we get it confirmed... what you gonna do about it?"

She stared at him. Hard.

"What you *mean* what am I going to do? I ain't havin' no abortion if that's what you're thinking," Alexis huffed.

"You fuckin' shittin' me, ma? I don't need this right now. My wife will fucking *divorce* me. The press will crucify me, another dumb athlete fuckin' up his life..." He felt panic rising. It hadn't been there when she'd dropped the bomb. He needed to think. This shit was controllable, whether he was the father, or not. There was a way of bringing things to a close. Make it seem natural. But not if she kept it and started running her mouth. If his wife found out... that would turn his whole fuckin' world to shit.

"You think I give a fuck about your wife, Devante?"

He started to pace the floor. The hotel room was pretty big, not luxury suite big, so it still only took him a dozen strides to get from one side to the other before he had to turn back again, mumbling, "I don't need this shit... I just don't fuckin' *need* it," to himself like some mantra.

His mind was clouded with confusion.

He had been the number one draft pick for the LA Lakers and everything was looking rosy. He'd ridden out the stress of getting hurt in his rookie year, and come back stronger than before. There was a two hundred-million-dollar contract on the table which brought everything he had ever wanted right along with it. And then some. He'd made it. He was Big Time. Capital B, Capital T. And he was fucked if he was going to screw it up for a piece of side ass.

Problem was, the contract had a morality clause, like all these things did these days. A get out of jail free card if he went full-on transphobic Trump-licking crazy like that Star Wars chick. Anything morally questionable, anything that put the team in a bad light, and made the money men think they needed to apologize to the wokerati, he could kiss his two hundred million bye bye.

If a fucking stripper had his baby and it came out, he was fucked, and not in the way that got him into this mess in the first place.

Two hundred fucking million.

Big Time.

"I don't know why you're treating me like this, Devante. I've always kept shit real with you." Alexis reminded him. He almost pitied her. But he pitied himself way more.

They heard a knock on the door.

"Finally," he grumbled, then flung open the door on his man, Crow. He stood there, tall and skinny; always there when he was needed, but still there when he wasn't. He handed over a brown bag with the test in it.

"Don't let that bitch play you, brah," Crow warned him. "You feel me? Be careful."

Crow had his own reasons for hating Alexis. He had tried to fuck her once, and she'd knocked him back, and not kindly. She'd laughed in his face. He was a scrawny, jet-black, crypt-keeper looking dude, and her laughter burned him to the core. He'd never forgiven her, and knowing Crow the way he did, Devante knew he never would. If there was anyone who knew how to hold a grudge, it was Crow.

"Your mama's a bitch!" She yelled over Devante's shoulder. Crow lunged, like he was gonna smack the next words right off her lips, but Devante pushed him back and shut the door.

He pulled the test out of the bag and held out the box and handed it over. First Step, just as she'd asked for. She snatched it out of his hand, picked up her purse, and headed for the bathroom.

Devante was right on her heels.

She tried to shut the door, but he pushed it open.

"Do you mind?" she huffed. "I don't need an audience to piss on a stick."

"Nah ma, I *need* to see."

"You need to *watch* me piss? Are you for real?"

Devante folded his arms across his chest. "You think I don't know the game? How I know you ain't got some pregnant girl piss in a bottle or another stick you gonna switch this one out with, and that why you were so set on the brand Crow brought?"

"I don't believe you, you're fuckin' whacked across the head stupid," Alexis spat as she stepped out of her Gucci boots. "But fine, why don't you get your dick in your hand and enjoy the show?" She stripped off her skin-tight catsuit, peeling out of the layers until she stood there butt-naked in the middle of the bathroom. Devante's dick got hard as a rock watching. No denying, her body was perfect. Flawless. And she had *the* best titties he had ever seen, even though, truth be told, he hadn't seen that many. Not in the flesh; not close enough to touch. Devante had been a tall and dorky growing up, with just one thing going for him; he was a hell of a basketball player. In high school, the bitches hadn't given him a second glance, but once he went pro things changed up. Now they screamed his name.

That's why Alexis had him so fucked up.

She was his dream girl come true. And wasn't it just like a

fool to have that dream become some twisted fuckin' nightmare shit.

"Happy now?" Alexis spat, cocking her hip to offer up a
peek at the camel toe between her legs.

"Just piss," he retorted, but his voice cracked from the
dryness of his lust.

Alexis held the stick under her as she squatted over the
toilet.

Goddamn, the bitch even pisses sexy, he thought to himself,
unable to take his eyes off her. He wanted to have his face
under that hot wet stream, looking up at her, licking...

When she finished, she sat on the toilet, and put the stick
on the bathroom counter.

Devante could hardly wait, but he forced himself to, pacing
the cramped room, muttering down the seconds, and despite
himself really wanting to take is dick out and... no, he couldn't
think like that. That was the kind of fucked up thinking that
got him in this mess.

Breathing hard, like he'd been playing a quarter, he picked
up the stick. His worst nightmare was confirmed in a line of
blue.

"Shit," he swore, slamming the stick down so hard the
damned thing broke—like the morality clause on his contract.

"Can I get dressed now?" Alexis hissed; her point proven.

He took one look at her pouting pussy and moved closer
until he was standing over her.

"Naw, hold up," he croaked, fumbling with his buckle.

Alexis pushed him away.

"Uh-uh, not after you tried to play me. Are you serious
right now?"

Devante whipped his dick out, pulling back on it so it
stood proud, hard.

"Come on Lexi, you know I take care of you," he crooned, pushing his dick up to her face, knowing she would open her mouth to him. He reached out to stroke her hair.

"Take care of me *how?* I ain't getting rid of my baby, if that what you thinking," she said, leaving him with no doubt that she was serious. She clamped her knees together and rested her elbows on her thighs, even though that put her lips even closer to his dick. It was an unfair situation; she'd had the time to give it thought, he'd only had a few minutes to wrap his head around it.

"Okay, ma, I'll make sure you're straight. You have my word. Just make sure I'm straight," he smirked, thinking, *Shit I'm rich, I can afford it.*

Alexis smirked, then kissed and worked the head of his dick, just like he'd known she would. Her tongue brought a moan of pleasure from Devante he couldn't have kept inside, even if he'd wanted to.

"So, what you want me to do with this?" She purred, rubbing his dick over her lips teasingly.

He was so hard it hurt.

"Come on baby, you know what I want."

She licked from his head to his balls. Another moan, almost pleading, this time desperate. Needing.

"Then give me what I *want.*"

"Anything," he said, and he damned near meant it. She could ask for anything and he'd give it to her. Almost anything.

"A hundred thou."

"You got it."

"A month."

He looked at her.

"A mo—"

That's all he got out before she deep-throated him, and

made him swallow any protest even as she swallowed him. Her head game was fierce. Sloppy and loud. Her throat constricted around him like a snake devouring its prey. It felt like a throbbing pussy it was that good. She was going to suck that hundred grand out of him whether he liked it or not.

And he definitely liked it.

Alexis slurped his dick like she was starring in a porno, and still managing to look up at him.

It didn't take long for Devante's whole body to begin to shiver, then explode.

"Mmm," Alexis moaned, swallowing every drop, not breaking eye contact with him for a pulse.

"You got me?" She purred.

"I got you, ma," he huffed, out of breath.

She smiled to herself, at least as contented as he was.

"Oh my God really? It was *that* easy? You just blew him?" Vita gasped in amazement. She leaned forward over the table eager to hear all the details.

"For sure, girl, I told you it would work!" Alexis said, feeling more pleased with herself than she could remember.

The bar was busy, noisy, but she was oblivious to anyone around them. She knew she should keep her voice down in case she as overheard, but all she could think about was how well everything had fallen into place, and how easy it had been.

"You weren't scared?" Vita asked.

"For what? Like I said, the only thing I was worried about was if he brought some cheap-ass brand, not First Step. If he did, I was done," she snickered, sipping on her wine, splashing a drop and licking it off the back of her hand.

She had set it all up.

All it had taken was a fake pregnancy test she bought off of the dark web. It worked like the real thing, but any kind of urine would trigger it to read positive. She guessed she wasn't the only one who used the trick for more than just a joke.

The rest was down to her head game and she was more than up to *that* job.

"Wow. A hundred grand. A month?"

"He agreed, but then I had his dick in my mouth at the time, and you know a man will say *anything* then. I figure he'll come through with at least twenty racks a month to keep me straight," Alexis reasoned. "And that's good enough."

"But what about when it's time to have the baby?"

"Did you feel that?" Alexis asked unable to take the smile from her face, and placed a hand on her stomach.

Vita frowned.

"Feel what?"

"I just had a miscarriage," Alexis joked and they both laughed, realizing only a few moments later that a couple of heads had turned in their direction.

"Shit, all that money. I guess you don't need this then, huh?" Vita said, lowering her voice and holding out a thumb drive.

Alexis snatched the memory drive from her quickly. She was not going to let that slip through her fingers.

"Hell yeah! I'm greedy. Bitch, I thought you knew," Alexis winked.

"Same," Vita said. "A hundred dollars a name."

Alexis put the thumb drive in her purse.

"Shit, all these identities are official, and I don't mind paying for quality."

Alexis looked around to make sure no one was watching, then slid Vita an envelope full of dead presidents. Vita slipped it into her purse, barely giving it a glance, and gave the widest smile.

"You're starting to trust me," Alexis remarked.

"What makes you think that?"

"You didn't count the money this time."

"Should I?"

"Don't I always come correct?"

Vita smiled and looked at her watch.

"I need to make a move. See you tonight?"

"No doubt," Alexis confirmed.

Vita kissed her on the cheek then walked away.

Alexis stayed in her seat and watched out of the window until the woman had got into her car. She felt that something wasn't quite right, but she tried to shake off the feeling. Everything was going well. Life was on the up. She finally had what she needed to produce the fake IDs that would open up phase two of her plan. She couldn't wait to get started. She could almost taste that success.

"Cheers to me," Alexis giggled, then drained the last of the wine in her glass.

COCO

"Thank you, Mrs. Washington, please come again," the cashier chimed, all sing-song as she handed Coco her bags, clearly delighted by the commission coming from them. And why shouldn't she? In her mind she'd almost certainly spent the dollars and cents she was expecting to receive.

She-it, I'll be back every day if it's this simple, Coco thought to herself.

She'd just torn the mall up.

She'd racked up a twelve-thousand-dollar account using a couple of cloned credit cards and now she was walking out of there loaded down with bags. Coco looked the part of the pampered housewife. That helped the scam. She wore a long, bone-straight black wig that went perfectly with her hazel eyes. She knew how striking she looked, and wanted people to notice and remember her, or at least remember what she looked like today. Big difference. Tomorrow she would look completely different.

And she had a whole new wardrobe to make that happen.

Coco strutted through the mall, turning heads left and

right. Enjoying it. She put on the strut. She owned the place. It was the kind of swagger that drove men crazy and annoyed the hell out of their partners. Women looked on enviously at her designer bags, knowing full well every one of them came from the most expensive stores in the mall.

She heard a voice call from behind her, "Excuse me, Mrs. Washington?"

She looked back and immediately wished she hadn't.

"Shit," She cursed under her breath, seeing another cashier from one of the previous stores she'd hit.

She was walking with two security guards—brutes who looked like they meant business. A few other shoppers were already turning to see what the fuss was all about, stepping aside like some sixth sense warned them trouble was about to go down.

"Mrs. Washington, can I speak with you for a moment please?" The cashier called.

Coco acted as if she couldn't hear.

She increased her stride without obviously accelerating, trying to look as if she was in a hurry to be somewhere else without it looking like she was running away.

When she looked back, she saw they'd sped up, too, matching her step. One of the security guards was on his walkie talkie. She didn't pause long enough to hear what he was saying. She already had a good idea what she was going to do, and she was going to stick with it.

"Fuck this," Coco spat, then took off running, no longer caring what anyone thought.

She needed to get out of there.

"Hey!" the other security guard hollered at her back, but Coco was like some teenager with her hands over her ears going *la la la* determined not to hear him.

She had zero intention of responding.

It was hard running in heels.

They were slowing her down, so she kicked them off mid-stride, and shot through the crowd.

The bags bounced against her legs. She bumped into shoppers who got too close, oblivious to what was going on. Coco didn't give a shit. She was in the zone, ignoring any discomfort, or anyone she had to push aside. She dipped and dodged through the crowd, security in hot pursuit. Her heart racing, her breathing quickly became labored. She was fuck-fit not run a marathon fit. Head down, she ran for the exit.

When she turned the corner, it was already blocked by three more security guards looking like they wanted to go to town on her black ass with their nightsticks.

"Shit!" she rasped, quickly changing direction. She almost lost her feet sliding like she was doing a black Risky Business, and hared down the right hand branch of shops with all their glittering prizes waiting to be won one fake visa card at a time.

She spotted a bathroom and smiled to herself.

Maybe she wasn't fucked after all.

She slipped inside, knowing the guards would hesitate before they followed her inside. They were men. That would buy her a few seconds. She could do a lot in a few seconds.

Coco quickly snatched of her wig and wig cap, revealing her close-cropped, autumn-tinted afro. She pulled down the leggings she'd pushed up under her skirt which she snatched off and bundled up, then slipped off her coat before she walked out of there, leaving the bags in the back of the stall. Not exactly Superwoman, but it only took a matter of seconds to become a whole new her. She walked out of there, head high, like she didn't have a care in the world as two female guards came barreling in.

"Oh, excuse me," Coco stammered as she walked straight into one of them.

The guards gave her the once over, but she didn't match the description of the woman they were looking for: long black hair, not an auburn natural, close cut. Leggings not a skirt. No coat. That was the secret of disguise. You could take stuff away for a quick change, it was so much harder to add stuff.

They slid in the bathroom and she slipped past them.

Coco walked straight past the guards who'd been chasing her seconds before, like she was a ghost, and hurried out of the mall.

Only when she reached her car did she dare release a sigh of relief, and almost as though the universe was mocking her, she heard a shout.

"There she is!"

But it was too late.

She slammed the car door, key in the ignition and gave them the finger as she screeched off. Coco saw them trying to write down her license plate, but the quick right she made blocked their view. They'd pick it up on CCTV later, but she'd changed plates so often she had no clue what car these ones even belonged to. She punched the accelerator and shot onto the busy street, barely missing a bus to a blare of horns, making a clean getaway.

"I can't believe this shit! Twelve grand! Twelve measly fuckin' grand. I'm gonna kill him! I'm gonna fuckin' kill him!" Coco screamed at the windshield, banging the heel of her hand on the steering wheel like it was his face and she was focused on mashing his nose to a pulp.

She might still have two thousand dollars' worth of jewelry in her purse, but that didn't change a thing. She was boiling.

She headed straight for Jose's apartment, coming to a screaming halt in front of the building.

Coco spared no more than a heartbeat to look back and double-check no one had tailed her, before she jumped out and headed inside.

He lived in the Dominican part of the city.

Her presence turned a few heads.

She flashed a smile at a couple old guys sitting outside enjoying the sun as it turned their skin to leather, before she went in. It was all for show. The smile disappeared the moment she was out of sight.

"This motherfucka's gonna get it," she mumbled under her breath, all the way up the elevator ride to Jose's floor.

She reached his apartment.

Coco hammered on the door so hard it stung her knuckles, each rap sounding like a gunshot.

"Who is it?" Jose barked from the other side of the door.

There were no sounds of movement inside.

"Open this fucking door!" She screeched, not caring who might hear her.

A couple of seconds later Coco heard the locks being released.

She pushed open the door the instant the handle stared to turn, slamming it open so hard she almost knocked him to the floor.

"Fuck is wrong with you?" Jose yelled, supporting himself against battered looking cupboard as he struggled to regain his balance.

He was a big dude, 240 pounds and 5'8", built like a bowling ball, but Coco was like a ball of fire, made to burn, and nothing was going to stand in her way.

"I want my fuckin' money, Jose! You gave me bad fuckin' cards!" She gritted.

"You crazy as hell! My shit was perfect!" He shot back. "You got made, that's on you."

"The fuck they were! I almost got popped!"

"Then bitch, you did something wrong! Or you hung around too long, got too greedy."

"Who you callin' a bitch?"

"You, bit—" was all he got out before Coco spat the razor from her mouth.

No one *ever* expected it, that was why it was her favorite weapon, even though it only gave one shot.

She'd learned the trick from a girl who'd been inside one of the toughest women's prisons. She'd shown Coco how to keep it in her mouth and still talk if she had to, without cutting herself. It was quite a trick but it was something that could only be kept up for so long, no matter how good you were with the old tongue. She'd slipped it into her mouth before she even knocked on the door. Like a girl scout. Prepared.

She didn't mean to kill him.

That certainly wasn't her intention.

She wanted to cut him, wound him, mark him, but murder wasn't on her mind.

She aimed for his face, but he moved, leaning away, as though anticipating the slash but getting it wrong. The angle exposed his neck and the razor bit into his jugular with deadly force. It cut so deep the blood spurted straight into her eye and splashed hot across her face.

"Aarrghhh!"

They both screamed, but for different reasons.

He screamed for his life, she screamed for her sight.

"I can't see!" she spat, stumbling around the room with both eyes closed.

Had she been able to open them, she would've seen the blood and the way Jose he was clutching at his neck and the sheer look of panic on his face. Instead, she rushed to the bathroom to rinse her face, desperate to wash the blood out of her eyes.

Coco turned on the faucet, scrubbing at her face until she could blink her eyes clear, then she washed away the last streak of red before drying with a towel.

Only then did she head back into the living room.

"Punk ass bitch! You must think shit is—" she started cursing, until she saw Jose motionless on the floor, lying in a slowly spreading pool of his own blood. It looked far too real.

She stopped short.

"Jose?"

No response. She kicked him; not hard, but enough to get a response. Or not.

"Jose?"

She knew then that there was no doubt. The next one Jose was gonna be talking to was an angel. Or a devil, more like, shit he'd pulled in his life, motherfucka was always going to hell. "Shit!"

Coco was no stranger to death; she had seen enough of it, but it familiarity didn't mitigate surprise.

She'd fucked up.

Her fingerprints would be all over the apartment.

She looked around, thought, then spat, "Fuck it," and ran into the bedroom.

She tossed his room until she found a box full of blank credit cards, an embosser, and a thumb drive.

It didn't take a genius to know that the drive held everything she need to make cloned cards. She'd stumbled on a gold mine and she had complete control over it; no need to pay a slice to a no-mark like Jose. Even if she had to pay someone to show her how to use the stuff, it would be a lot less than Jose would have skimmed her for.

"This is gonna be fun."

Beneath the bed, she found a duffel bag and was about to drop her haul into it which she realized that there were bundles of British ten pound notes.

"What the fuck?" She whispered to herself, peeling one of the bills off the bundle to take a closer look at it. She had no idea what Jose was doing with this, and even though she'd never been outside the boroughs, she as pretty damned sure that there was something wrong about it. There were only two possible explanations. Either the money was stolen, or it was counterfeit. Either way, she had zero clue what she could do with the stash, but it was sure as fuck no use to Jose.

Not anymore.

She didn't want to leave fingerprints or any lingering memory of her presence on people's mind, and wished now that she hadn't smiled at the two old guys outside.

She decided that the best thing to do might be to burn the place down.

It might be extreme, but it would cover up all kinds of things, including the fact that Jose's death hadn't been completely accidental.

She gave the room one last glance around, then remembered Jose's fancy watch.

"Sorry Jose," she told the corpse, taking the twenty-thousand-dollar Rolex off his wrist. "But I need it more than you do."

She went to take off the gold chain he wore around his neck.

It was no good to him, either, but it caught on something.

She thought it might be his chest hairs, so she tugged at his shirt.

She was more than a little surprised when it came free and what came with it; he was wearing a wire.

Her heart jumped in her throat.

She covered her mouth to keep from crying out.

Coco scrambled away from the wire and the corpse, as if it were a camera someone could be watching her through, not just a microphone.

Jose had been wearing a wire.

Jose was a fucking *informant*.

Jose was dead.

She had killed him while he was wired, and someone, somewhere, had heard her do it.

"Fuck."

She tried to ignore the hammering in her chest, replaying their conversation in her head. She couldn't remember if he'd used her name.

Had he?

"Fuck."

All Coco heard was the slamming of a gavel somewhere in her near future. It was an unpleasant sound.

She expected the feds to bust in at any moment. She'd already taken the door down for them.

When they didn't, she gathered herself, grabbed her score, and headed for the door, deciding not to burn the building down.

She wiped down everything she had touched, or even

thought she might have touched, then left, taking the stairs instead of the elevator.

With every step she expected to hear someone bark, "Freeze!" but when she didn't—and she made it to the car, calming herself before driving off, she whispered, "Thank God," to the Big Guy and headed for the highway.

JORDAN

"Do you remember talking to me in the hospital?" Myers asked.

"Vaguely," Jordon answered, the truth, the whole truth and nothing but.

"Vaguely? You seem especially...coherent," Myers pointed out. There was a knowing smirk on his lips.

He didn't feel like her friend anymore.

"My memory comes and goes. I'm sorry. I remember someone coming to see me, but there were people in and out all the time."

Myers nodded, keeping steady eye contact.

"I can appreciate that. Okay, how about you tell me about the accident? Talk me through it."

"I can't. It's not that I don't want to. I just don't remember anything about it." He didn't seem surprised, but then nothing seemed to surprise him. He was leading her through this to where he needed her to go for the jury. She just didn't know where that was.

"Does the name Raymond James mean anything to you?"

"Yes. But only because you have asked me about him before. I still don't know who he is," Jordan replied. She felt the urge to fidget in her chair but resisted, knowing how that would look to the twelve men and women watching her.

"What about his nickname, Spaz?"

"No." She shook her head. "That means nothing to me."

He paused for a moment, but didn't take his eyes off her.

He tried another name. "Victor Jefferson, also known as Cool V? You must have heard of him?"

This time she flinched. She couldn't help it.

"Yes. Again. But only what you've told me."

"Which is?"

"You told me he's my husband," she admitted, with no sign of recognition on her face.

Myers took off his glasses and wiped them clean, using his tie.

"Well, Mrs. Jefferson, that's a lot of stuff you don't remember, so perhaps you'd like to tell the court what you *do* remember?"

Jordan looked at him for a beat, took a deep breath, then closed her eyes... There were things she *could* tell him, things that had happened recently, but she still couldn't tell him what he really wanted to know: about the accident.

Bullets breezed past her ears like sinister whispers of death. She kept on running, head down, driving herself on as fast as she could. Her legs blazed with sinister fire. She gasped for breath like it was the last one she was sucking down into her lungs.

"Faster!" Minx urged her.

Jordan's mind was frazzled.

She hadn't been out of the hospital a day and she was already being chased and shot at?

She'd been walking down the street, trying to get her bearings in what was essentially a brand new city to her, when out of nowhere a van skidded up, panel doors sliding open as thugs inside tried to snatch her of the street.

If it hadn't been for Minx—quick on her feet and quick inside her head—grabbing a hot cup of coffee out of the hand of a man on the sidewalk and flinging it in the face of her would be kidnapper, Jordan would have been in the back of the van, heading God knows where.

At least like this she had a chance, which was more than she would have had in that van.

It had all happened so incredibly quickly; he'd screamed as the scalding hot coffee burned at his flesh. Minx had yelled, "RUN!" And she'd took off like the devil knew she was dead and had come for her soul, streaking down the street like she was still on the track team. She jetted down the stone steps into the piss-stinking subway entrance, pushing people aside. Her pursuers were unfettered by the spectacle they were making chasing her.

"Get on the train," Minx huffed, struggling to catch her breath.

"Are you crazy? We'll be trapped!" Jordan protested.

"Trust me."

With no alternative, Jordan jumped on the train as it rolled into the station, pushing through the swam of people to get into the tin can. It was way too crowded inside bodies pressed too tight against each other.

One of those bible thumpers was clearing his throat in the middle of the crowd and asking everyone if they'd made their peace with God. Why? Because if they hadn't they were going to hell. The first time she'd heard someone like him running that schtick she'd thought someone was going to put a cap in their ass...

That stopped her short.

Was it a flash of memory or a moment of obvious cause and effect? Reach into a bag on a crowded subway train, ask if people were going to hell... get shot?

She dared to risk a look back and saw her pursuers getting on board.

"Keep moving," Minx urged, pushing her forward until they reached the end of the carriage.

The last few passengers were getting on.

With the train doors about to close, Minx shouted, "Now!" And lunged forward, barreling out onto the platform, Jordan a step behind her, as the doors slammed closed, trapping her pursuers on the train.

Jordan looked at them as they glowered at her, their faces pressed against the glass panel of the door.

"What I tell you? Works every time," Minx snickered.

"Why were they shooting at you?" Jordan wanted to know.

"No time for all that. Those motherfuckers will already be calling for the van to cover the entrance. We have to go," Minx remarked. "On our feet or in a box. Only choices right now"

Jordan knew she was right. She hurried out of the station and kept going, running down street after faceless street, weaving through walkers. That was the beauty of the city; everyone was rushing to get to where they were going, so they never looked up.

Finally, they arrived at what looked like a boarding house.

"This place is a shithole," Jordan spat contemptuously.

"You got a room at the Waldorf we can use?" Minx quipped. "I'm all for a bit of luxury, sister. Otherwise, it's this."

Jorden looked around, but kept her mouth shut.

The place had been a hotel years ago. Since then, it gone through a painful transition into a brothel, then a homeless shelter, and now it was a combination of the two. There was no telling how the place was still standing. Maybe the roaches were all that kept it upright?

"Hey there, pretty lady. Where've you been the last few days?" A toothless old beggar cackled at Minx as she blew him a kiss.

"Hospital, Charlie. Any messages?"

"Expecting any?" Charlie answered.

"Not if I'm lucky," Minx replied.

"Then you one lucky lady."

She led the way up the stairs to the third floor.

"Doesn't the elevator work?" Jordan huffed.

"Trust me, you *don't* want to get stuck in that thing," Minx warned. "Reeks of piss, got more cracks in it than most of the ho's in this place, and breaks down at least twice a day."

The room had no bathroom; just a bed, a rickety looking table held together by gum, and a view of the brick wall of the building opposite, no more than six feet across from her window.

Directly opposite, there was another window.

"They can see straight in here," Jordan said, looking at the other window in something akin to horror.

"I've got nothing to hide, plus, it ain't like they gonna get a show from us," Minx said with a knowing grin, then laughed. "It's abandoned. Don't worry."

Jordan sank down onto the bed.

She hated the fact that she couldn't remember *anything*

about her past. Even the simple stuff like: *where she was from, who she had been, if she had any family? Did she have kids? Were her parents still alive, and if so, were they close? And who had been on the bike with her?* If it had been her husband, surely the police would have said, if only to see how she reacted?

All she had were those painful memories of her mother.

"Hey, don't worry. Like the doc said, you never know with head trauma. Your memory could come back tomorrow, like that," Minx snapped her fingers, sounding optimistic.

"Or never," Jordan countered, sourly, then added, "What's your story?"

"Long."

"We got time. Especially if it'll help me understand why those guys wanted to kill you," Jordan said, realizing just how little she knew about her new partner in crime.

"Look, if I tell you, you have to swear not to say anything to anybody," Minx said firmly. "I'm serious about that. I'm dealing with enough shit as it is."

"I won't," Jordan said, already starting to dread what she might be about to hear.

"Swear?"

"I swear."

"I like your face, so I guess I can trust you." Minx smiled, her own hard-edged face softening a little.

Jordan laughed but she wasn't sure why.

Minx got down on her hands and knees and pulled a suitcase out from under the bed, then unzipped it.

It was full of money.

"Jesus fucking God! How much?"

"Close to three million dollars," Minx answered. "I counted it."

Jordan couldn't believe her eyes. She'd never seen anything close to that much money in her life.

Then she noticed something else.

"They're all hundred-dollar bills."

Minx smiled.

"Yup. They're also counterfeit."

"What? How do you know?"

Minx zipped the suitcase up and pushed it back under the bed.

"Bottom line is I'm rich—on fake paper—but I can't spend a dime until I make them real."

"And that's why they are trying to kill you? Whose money is it?"

"It doesn't matter."

"But if whoever it is, is shooting at you—"

"Then I've got him right where I want him," Minx laughed, and it was the oddest sound in the world.

"I—I don't understand," Jordan admitted.

"You don't have to, sister. The only question I have, do you want to help me go from fake-paper rich to real rich?"

Jordan thought about it.

In a city where she didn't know a soul, not even herself, Minx was all she had. Even if she was a marked woman.

"I guess I don't have a choice."

"You do. But, you won't regret it. I'll let you in on this lick, but you better not try and cross me. You feel me? If you get any dumb fuck ideas, I'll have to kill you."

Jordan could tell she wasn't joking.

"I won't."

"Okay, one last thing and this one is kinda important. Have you ever stripped before?"

"Stripped?"

"Minx! Where the *fuck* you been? I see you one week, you disappear the next?" Big Bobby grunted, spit flying from his fat ass lips.

Black and ugly as ever, fit Bobby perfectly, but since he managed the strip club and had plenty of money, bitches flocked around him like he was some kind of pussy magnet.

"I was in the hospital. Did you want me bleeding all over the place?" Minx sassed.

"Hell no! And you better be healed! Don't want some John trying to claim his dollar bills back 'coz you bleed on them. Now get your ass out there and work, girl, there's money needing to be parted from all those horn dogs."

Big Bobby stormed off without a backward glance.

"Don't worry about him. His bark is way worse than his bite," Minx promised.

"Is he the owner?" Jordan asked, trying to understand the lie of this strange land they'd just walked into.

"The manager. But he's a pushover. Give him head and he kicks like an ATM."

"I'm not giving head," Jordan balked.

"If the price is right you will," Minx shot back. "Trust me. We all do in the end."

Jordan looked around, gawking at her surroundings, but trying not to let it show. She watched the girls saunter around in various stages of naked. Titties jiggling, and ass everywhere. Her own outfit didn't leave much to the imagination. She wore a thong that accentuated her shapely hips and ass, and a bustier that made her c-cups look delectable.

"Damn li'l mama, I ain't seen you befo'. What's your name?"

Jordan heard the voice, then turned around to see who it belonged to.

She couldn't lie, he was definitely fine. He reminded her of Lance Gross, with his smooth chocolate skin and wavy hair.

"Jordan."

"Damn, do you flow like the river Jordan? If so, baptize me," he winked, giving her a dimpled smile. "So, how about a dance?" he asked, teasing up a twenty dollar bill.

Jordan walked up to him and took the bill.

"I—um—This is my first time," she stuttered. "Be gentle."

"A virgin huh? Why don'tchu come on over and let daddy pop your cherry?"

She straddled his lap facing away.

She caught her own reflection in the mirror stretching along the opposite wall. She saw Minx's reflection looking back at her. Her smile gave her confidence, and holding her gaze, Jordan began to work her hips, mimicking Minx's moves as she gave her first lap dance, grinding. It felt natural. Like she might have done it a thousand times before, though she could not imagine having done it in a place like *this*.

"Mmm, you nice. You don't move like no virgin," he joked.

"You like that?" Jordan purred, feeling a thrill at his appreciation.

"Like it? Here's twenty more. Keep going for another song. That's how much I like it, l'il mama."

Jordan leaned over and grabbed her ankles as she started grinding on his lap.

"Jordan, right?"

"Yes."

"You look kinda familiar. Don't I know you?"

Her breath caught in her throat, but she kept working his hard-on, feeling it stiff against her.

"I don't know. Do you?"

Deep down, she hoped that he did, and that he could tell her *something* about herself. Evan the smallest thing might trigger a new memory.

"I would love to get to know you. My name is David."

"Nice meeting you, David."

The second song ended and Jordan stood up.

David took her hand.

"I know you got to work, but I would like to see you again. When the time isn't borrowed," he requested smoothly.

"I don't know, I'd rather—"

David slipped his card in her hand, then curled her fingers around it.

"At least keep the card. The offer stands," he winked then walked off.

Jordan watched him stride away.

She couldn't help it.

She was definitely feeling his swag.

She had all but decided to call when she looked at the card.

What she read damn-near took her breath away.

ALEXIS

"Who's the new bitch?" Alexis asked, glaring across the club.

"Minx? Lil Mix? Something like that. I don't know and to be honest, I don't care. I got my own problems," Coco spat as she downed her drink.

Her mind was still on Jose's dead body, and the rats that were probably chowing down on him like he was rat thanksgiving. She'd been on edge ever since she'd left his apartment, expecting the Feds to come down on her any moment.

Alexis was never one to miss anything.

She eyed her closely.

"What's wrong with you? Every two seconds you checkin' over your shoulder, all tense and shit. You expecting someone?"

"Nothing," Coco hissed.

"Bullshit," Alexis shot back.

"What's up Lex? Can a nigg—"

"I'm busy," Alexis snapped at the tall, dark dude who was approaching her.

She knew him well and knew he didn't have any real money so she ran her hot and cold game on him. Sometimes, usually on the quiet days when Johns were a little thin on the ground, she'd be all over him. Other days, when there were richer pickings to be had, she wouldn't give him the time of day. This kept him off balance, so when she did give him attention, he kicked like a slot machine to keep it.

Her game was tight as fish pussy. Waterproof.

He walked off like a spurned puppy, tail between his legs, but just like a dog he'd be back again soon enough. Maybe not today, though. He was sharp enough not to take two kickings in one day.

"Back to you. And bitch, don't lie to me," Alexis sassed, nodding for the bartender to bring them both another drink.

Coco shook her head, then mumbled, "I need to get out of town."

Alexis's eyebrow arched.

"Why?"

Coco looked around.

"Some crazy shit happened, all right? I just need to bounce."

"Then go."

"It ain't that simple. My pockets ain't right," Coco admitted.

She was cash broke.

She had the jewelry she could pawn and the equipment to make herself some credit cards thanks to the stuff she'd lifted from Jose's crib, but that was about it. To make any money out of that would take time. She'd have to learn how to use it all, or find someone who could. Even then there was no guarantee that those cards would work any better than the last batch had.

Problem was, time was one thing she didn't have.

"How much you need," Alexis asked, reeling her in.

Coco shrugged. "Maybe twenty. At least ten."

"What happened to your credit card scam?"

"It's too hot," Coco answered, like the best lies there was a shit load of truth in it. There was no need to go into all the details. She certainly didn't need to tell her about the dead body she'd got on her hands.

Alexis knew there was more to it than Coco was letting on. She intended to get to the bottom of it all. There was always some kind of advantage to be had in knowing someone else's secrets, and Alexis was always hunting for that angle. It was her nature, like the scorpion.

"What if I could help you?"

Coco looked at her skeptically.

"You help me? Bitch, what's in it for you?" Coco asked flat out. She knew that Alexis never did *anything* purely out of the kindness of her twisted black little heart.

"You don't need to worry about that. All you need to know is I can get you twenty-five-hundred. If you tell me who you really are. Nobody knows anything about you, and I'm damned sure that Coco ain't your real name. I might need it for something I've got going on."

"Hell no."

Alexis shrugged. "No biggie."

Coco thought about it for a moment. Her credit was shot, she didn't have a bank account. So what did she *really* have to lose?

"What is it? Income tax scam?" Coco asked.

Alexis suppressed her smile. "I've got a plug at H&R bank."

"Twenty-five-hundred?"

"Upfront."

Coco sighed.

"Make it happen."

"Say no more."

Alexis handed the other woman her phone.

"Put your social in."

Coco balked, shaking her head no. "Not until I get my money."

"No babes, it doesn't work like that. Info first. I'll have your money ready for you in a couple of days."

Coco dead-eyed Alexis. "Don't play with me, Lexi."

"Two days. Word."

"Fine. But if you're fucking with me..." Coco plugged her social security number into Alexis's phone before she handed it back. "Two days, no more. You don't want to find out what I'm capable of."

Alexis was no killer. The dead-eyed look Coco gave her shook her to the core, but she did well not to show it.

"You'll get your money," she fronted, then stood up, turned her back and walked away.

Her eyes fell on Minx. The woman was working the pole. All the Trick's, Ballers and Simp's in the room fixated by her serpent dance, as she worked her way through her pole tricks, including the guy she'd just blown off. All the girls were different. Some offered extras, other the true girlfriend experience, couch dances, air dances, anything to make it rain. It was a high mileage joint, and Alexis didn't like the idea of fresh competition. In the dark part of her heart she prepared for battle.

She dialed a number as she headed into the bathroom.

As soon as the voice came on the other end of the line she said, "I got one."

VITA

"Send me the deets. I'm deep in the middle of something right now," Vita replied, then hung up without waiting for a reply.

She stood in the middle of Jose's living room watching as three rats gnawed away at his corpse, high on his meat and oblivious to her presence. His body was beginning to get that special dead-man reek. Or maybe she was imagining it. She could barely breathe. This wasn't her first body. She could handle it. The rats, she wasn't so keen on, but as long as they weren't interested in her she was happy to let them feed.

"Shit," she spat, then headed for the bedroom.

She crossed the room, opening the closet and riffling through the shit inside, well aware of what wasn't.

"Figures as much," she stated, calm though she was boiling inside. It was an effort not to tear the place apart in a rage.

By the smell, the decomposition and the that the flies eggs had begun to hatch, she figured the body had been in the apartment for several days, and would have stayed undiscovered if she hadn't called in to check on him.

Jose didn't have many friends, or a social life.

Well, not anymore, anyway.

The way this city is, the poor bastard could lie here forever without anyone stumbling on him as long as the rent's paid up, she thought to herself. She shut the door with a handkerchief over her hand.

"Not my problem," she mumbled to herself. All it would take was one call and it would happily become someone else's.

The wire he'd taped to him was still in place, and whoever had killed him had seen it.

Deciding that discretion was called for, she removed it and slipped it into her bag. She didn't need any more questions being asked when the body was discovered. There would be more than enough already.

She headed for the stairs.

Outside, she scanned the block, her eyes looking for clues, because they were always there if you knew where to look. There would be *something* here to help her figure out what the ever-loving fuck had happened.

Then she saw it.

Vita headed across the street to a store two blocks from the corner. It was a jewelry store, but she wasn't going there to buy shiny things. Vita walked in, a professional smile on her face as she approached the woman behind the counter.

"Excuse me," she smoothed. "Are you the manager?"

The petite white woman flashed a too-white smile and said, "Why yes, is everything ok?"

"Could I trouble you for a moment of your time?" Vita said.

"Well. We were just about to close,"

"Shouldn't take too long, I promise," Vita flipped open her wallet to reveal a badge and ID.

"Federal Agent Vita Lewis."

The woman's smile remained fixed in place, but a ghost of panic flickered across her face. Obviously, she'd got her secrets. Vita wasn't interested in any of them. The owner turned to a short Hispanic woman, and said something to her softly in Spanish. She turned back to Vita, all smiles, and said, "This way, please," lifting the counter.

Vita followed her into a small office in the back.

It looked to be a well-organized set up. There was a computer monitor on the desk. What she couldn't see was a single scrap of paper. Maybe the woman always worked like this, or more likely those couple of seconds and whispered words had sent her assistant scurrying through to sweep everything away into a desk drawer.

"Is there a problem officer?"

"Not with you, Ms.—,"

"Edmanos," she said.

"I'm really hoping to get a look at any footage you might have of the street outside the store covering the last few days. I noticed you have a surveillance camera, I'm hoping it might have picked up something," Vita explained.

Edmanos breathed an obvious sigh of relief.

"Oh *that*? Well, of course. Anything to help the law."

She turned to her surveillance monitor and keyed in short password string. A moment later Edmanos pulled up images of the street. They weren't the best quality, and not the highest resolution, but the camera caught the front of the building perfectly.

She looked at the time stamp running across the bottom corner of the screen, and made a guess based on the smell and state of decomposition that Jose had been dead for three days, maybe four. No longer than that because the rats would have done a lot more damage to the corpse.

"Could you spool back one more day?"

"Of course."

It took twenty minutes of fast forwarding through images, but it was there: a woman pulled up to the building and got out of her car. Vita's eyes remained glued to the footage, looking for a flicker of shadow. Anything to say the woman had gone out the back, or that this wasn't what it seemed. Ten minutes later, the same woman hurried out of the building, clutching a large day bag.

Got you, Vita thought.

She didn't recognize the face. That wasn't a big thing. She had the resources to find out who she was. She was too striking for no-one to recognize her mugshot.

"Do you think I could get a copy of this?"

"Of course," Edmanos answered.

Vita looked at the woman, caught frozen in time as she looked over her shoulder, worry carved deep into that gorgeous face.

Yeah look back over your shoulder, sugar. I'm here, you just don't know it yet, Vita promised.

JORDAN

"The police? Oh, hells no!" Minx spat, bitterly. "Are you out of your mind?"

"But I *like* him. He was *nice* to me," Jordan protested.

"Of course he was nice to you. He wants some pussy," Minx pointed out. "They're always nice when they think there's a way to get at that honey. Fuck him. And by that I mean *don't* fuck him. We've got way too much going on to have the police hanging around."

Jordan bristled.

"*We* ain't got nothing going on. *You've* too much going on."

"And you're with me, or did you forget? You got somewhere else to go?"

Jordan dropped her head.

"I just like him. Is that so wrong?"

Minx sighed hard, not bothering to hide her exasperation.

"Look, I know you want to get to know him, and I'm sure he's one cute motherfucker, just the kinda boy you wanna take home to mom, but now just isn't the time. You get that right? Just give me a little time to put this move together, then, if you want to holler at ol' boy, be my guest. Deal?" Minx offered. "He'll still be around. I can promise you that."

Jordan brightened.

"Deal."

"Now...I need to deal with *her*," Minx sneered menacingly.

Alexis was feeling buzzed as she shuffled her way into the bathroom.

Her mind had already moved onto the hot date she'd just arranged with one of her Trick's.

No reason not to mix business with pleasure as far as she was concerned. It wasn't like she was offering extras, this was off the clock.

"*Bands make her dance*," she sing-songed playfully as she headed into the stall.

That was the last thing she said before she felt the hand grab a fistful of her hair and slam her face into the wall.

Alexis screamed, pain filling her head as blood gushed from her nose. The scream was lost in the relentless drum and bass of the stage area.

"Bitch, don't holla now!" Minx growled, voice like a panther on the prowl. She spun Alexis around to face her, then smacked the fire out of her.

"You got a problem with me?" Minx demanded, right up in her grille.

"I don't even know you!" Alexis shrieked, struggling to focus.

"You right. You don't know me. But you been eyein' me like you do! Now, I ask you again: do you have a problem with me?"

Minx grinned, then punctuated her words with another vicious slap.

"No!" Alexis squealed.

Minx punched her in the stomach hard enough to double the other woman over.

Minx dropped her to her knees.

Then, using the purchase she had with her hair, held Alexis's head in the toilet bowl, just inches away from the piss and a bloody maxi pad floating so close to her face.

"You're the type of bitch I would've raped in prison," Minx snarled.

"Please!"

"You think I don't *know* what you doing? The scams you're runnin'? I know. And you gonna cut me in on everything and then a little later I'm gonna put you down on an even bigger scam, you feel me?"

"Oh—*sniff*—okay," Alexis sopped.

"*And*," Minx added, getting close to her ear, "you're gonna be *my* bitch."

Alexis didn't respond.

Minx forced her face down until the piss-stained pad touched her nose.

"Say it or drink, your choice."

"I'll be your bitch! I swear to fucking god I will," Alexis blurted out.

Minx let Alexis go.

"Smart girl."

Alexis sank back against the stall wall, gasping for air, and stared up at Minx with pure fear in her eyes.

"Remember this because if you *ever* get out of line I'll cut your goddamned throat. And you won't see me coming."

Alexis head bobbed up and down like it was loose on her neck.

Minx playfully slapped her, a smile on her face.

"Good, now get yourself cleaned up. You've got a hot date, remember?"

ALEXIS

Alexis sat on the floor of the stall, sobbing as she struggled to clear her head. She'd never been so scared in her life. Her heart pounded a mile a minute. It even hurt to breathe. Her breastbone screamed from where it had been pressed so brutally hard up against the toilet seat.

She forced herself to get to her feet, closing her eyes for a second as the world spun, then staggered over to the mirror.

When she looked at herself, she saw the blood under her nose, and felt another crashing wave of pain.

"Shit," she spat, wringing out a wet tissue that she used to dab away the blood.

That bitch is crazy, Alexis thought to herself.

She'd looked in Minx's eyes and seen a madness dancing in them, like she had a demon in her. She'd heard Minx say she had been to prison. She shuddered to think what would've happened if they had met inside.

Alexis may've been working cons, but there was no way she was been ready for a bitch like Minx. She was going to play her game, no choice about that, but in the end, Alexis knew she had the upper hand because she had the ace...

Darla.

"Two for the price of one, huh?" KB cackled as he eyed Minx and Alexis side by side.

"Excuse *you*? Ain't shit free here, baby," Minx sassed. "You get double, you pay double."

"Naw, naw, just a figure of speech. I got plenty of money," he bragged, pulling out two rolls of bills.

"Then I got plenty of time," Minx winked, liking the thickness of all his rolls.

KB smiled cockily, holding the keycard up to the lock and letting them into the party room of his hotel suite.

It was huge, but that was only to be expected.

Everything KB did was big.

He was a major player. A music producer with multiple hits behind him. In demand because he had the Midas touch. And he didn't care who knew how successful he was. When he spent, he splurged, and money bought everything he desired. Simple as that.

Alexis had first met him when she had been with Devante at the Superbowl. They'd exchanged numbers on the low, and whenever he was in town, he hit Alexis up to party.

Alexis hated having to split the pot with Minx, but truth was she was scared to tell her no. That crazy bitch had a way of just taking what she wanted, and you getting hurt in the process if you tried to say no.

"You ladies come on in and get comfortable," KB said.

Minx slipped off her halter top, freeing her luscious

curves without waiting for any more invitation. Alexis was forced to admit, the girl had the goods *and* she knew how to use them.

"I ain't come here to get comfortable. I came to bone," Minx cooed, grabbing Alexis around the wrist, pulling her close.

She tongued her down.

KB was hooked. He stood there, grinning as he watched the show.

"We got us an alpha bitch in the house," he cackled. "I *like* it." He stretched that last like out for seconds, savoring it on his tongue just as Minx was savoring Alexis.

Alexis wasn't into women, not her bag, but on stage she could fake it.

At that moment, though, knowing what would happen if she went against the tide, she did what she had to do and just went with the flow.

Minx broke the kiss long enough to turn to KB and breathe, "Nigga, pop that bottle," like they were the sexiest words in the language.

KB grabbed the Ace of Spades and opened it, allowing the bubble to spill over.

He poured some onto Minx's breasts, lapping the sparkling suds up, and kissed his way across her curves.

"Maybe a glass would be better," Minx giggled. "You'd make less mess."

He grabbed three glasses and filled them with champagne.

As soon as he had done it, Minx covered his mouth with hers, sliding her tongue in deep inside, tender for a moment, like there was a real connection. She could sell herself like that. Sell the lie. He pulled her close and palmed her ass. KB was in heaven, and way too preoccupied to notice Minx breaking open a pill capsule with one hand, deftly dumping the white powder into his drink.

But Alexis did.

What the fuck is this basic bitch up to? she thought to herself.

When Minx broke the kiss, she saw Alexis looking at her. Minx winked before she handed KB his glass.

"Drink up," she urged, finger to her lips. "I don't know about you, but these bubbles always get me in the mood."

He didn't need telling twice.

He downed his drink in a single gulp, then tossed the glass aside.

"Now, how 'bout I drink you?" He growled, grabbing for Minx again.

She brushed his hands off, playfully.

"First, me and my girl here, we wanna to put on a show, just for you," Minx said, "We know what you like."

"And what do I like?"

She pull an extra-long dildo out of her bag.

"Alexis, film this."

Alexis knew Minx was setting something up, so didn't hesitate, even at the sight of the dildo. She took her phone out and started recording. It would have been nice if she'd told her in advance, though.

"Damn," KB laughed. "What you gonna *do* with that?"

Minx pulled Alexis to her.

"What do you think?" Minx replied, gazing into Alexis' eyes.

"I can't. It's too big," Alexis whined, but the look in Minx's eyes said her pleas were useless. This was going to happen whether she wanted it or not.

"Take off your clothes...now," Minx ordered her.

Alexis pulled down her skirt to reveal her phat ass was pantiless.

KB grabbed his dick.

"That's what I'm talkin' about. Take that pussy," he said, his voice slurring.

Minx gazed at Alexis' flawless body. Minx loved to look at a woman's body. Especially one as shapely as Alexis'.

"Get on your knees," Minx ordered softly.

Slowly, Alexis lowered herself to her knees.

"Daaaaaaaamn woman," KB groaned, barely able to keep his eyes open.

A moment later he slumped over on his bed.

"Start recording," Minx told her, and less than a minute later he was moaning in pain.

"Take it deep," Minx said, deepening her voice to sound like a man.

———

"Forward the video to his phone, but we're taking everything else."

Alexis' eyes grew huge as the dollar bills Minx was imagining. "Are you crazy? KB's whole team is gansta!" And a beat later, the realization. "He knows who I am. He knows how to find me."

"Which makes it that much better. What gangsta wants to be seen with a dildo up his ass?" Minx smiled. "And let's be honest, on that little snatch of homemade porn it looks like another guy deep dicking him, don't it?"

Alexis thought about it, then despite herself, smiled.

"Damn, you slick, sister."

They took his jewelry, his money, and even his clothes,

before leaving him alone with the dildo like it was some sort of prize.

———————

"You missed all the fun, "Minx said, as she collapsed back onto her own bed.

"I was asleep," Jordan answered.

"Be real, you were *pouting*," Minx shot back knowingly. She crossed her hands behind her head and smiled up at the ceiling in the dark, satisfied.

"No, I wasn't."

"You're a lousy liar, even when I can't see your face. We both know you were pouting because you can't have your little cop."

Silence.

"You know I'm right."

"You just want to corner me," Jordan remarked.

"Tell me this, Jay-Jay, do you really want the cop *that* bad?"

"Yeah."

"Okay, one condition."

"What?"

"I get some first."

"You're out of your mind."

"Think of it as marking my territory," Minx urged. Running her hand up her thigh, moving towards that sweet vee. "It'll be fun. Promise. You know you want to. I know you got the beast in you. He *is* cute though, so how 'bout we fuck him together, you and me? What's yours is mine?"

"I—" Jordan's back arched, reacting to her touch.

"—Say yes."

COCO

Coco sat on her bed, staring down at the stacks of British pounds bundled up, convinced that they were counterfeit rather than stolen.

What the fuck am I going to do with this shit? She asked herself. It was a lot more than a sixty-four thousand dollar question. If she could find a way of passing it on, everything would be golden. But if not? It was a hold lot of nothing.

Problem was, there was nowhere in America she could get it to pay out...or at least so she thought. Nowhere was like never, it only took one to make it a lie.

Her thoughts were interrupted by the buzz vibration of her phone ringing on silent.

She checked the screen to see it was her boy, Ray.

"What's up, Ray?" She answered, realizing there probably wasn't a whole heap of enthusiasm in her voice.

"What's wrong with you?" He said, picking up on it right away. "You sound like somebody died."

"Naw, shit just twisted."

"Then I'm right on time. I got a lick if you want in."

Her ears perked up. "A lick?" Coco echoed.

"No doubt. And you *just* the person I need to help me get it off. You down?" Ray asked.

"You already know it," Coco smirked.

"I'm on my way."

Click.

Coco's spirits picked up like a coke hit, straight into the rush. Ray always had a sweet scheme set up. The last time they ran a scam together, Coco made eighteen thousand off of credit cards.

There'd been a spell where Ray had worked at a high-end luxury store in the mall. The place sold all the brands and offered up complimentary bubbles while they waited to take your bills. He'd made pretty good commission, but seeing the sheer number of rich kids come in and spend thousands and on some occasions hundreds of thousands got to him. The division of wealth got under his skin. He was busting a gut for these dicks and getting nothing for it, comparatively. He wanted more. He wanted to live like them. It was a seductive image, that lifestyle, like a line of china white for an addict in withdrawal, and he was determined to get it by any means possible; including skimming.

The technology was there, and cheap enough to get his hands on, he just needed to work a few contacts. Less than a week after committing to it, he was inserting a modified microchip skimmer into the credit card reader.

It was as simple as that.

The microchip copied all of the card's information, including the PIN as the customer keyed it in, and the signature confirmation image. All he needed to do was switch the chip out every couple of shifts and put the credit card information on blank cards. The toughest thing after that was working out what he wanted to buy.

Ray was a gregarious dude. He made friends easily. A smile, a few funny words and suddenly he was besties with a lot of the employees from other stores. And that was when the magic happened. He got in with guys at different stores in the mall, cutting them in on the action if they'd run the scam in their own stores. There were enough disgruntled minimum wage slaves who wanted to even things up and sick of seeing these dumb shit white folks hoarding all the wealth and treating them like characters from Roots. It was all about getting ahead, being smarter than the marks.

In the beginning they'd concentrated on buying clothes, because like the old saying went, the clothes made the man, then they moved on to designer *everything*.

When Ray pulled up, he hadn't even made it out of the car before Coco was at the door.

"Goddamn, you *thirsty*," he remarked with a chuckle as Coco climbed in.

"I told you shit is twisted. I need to make a grip quick so I can slide," Coco told him.

"Bad shit?" That tripped his radar.

"Naw, my grandma in Atlanta is sick," she lied. She was a good liar. Better than most at least. She sold it without missing a beat.

"Sorry to hear tha," Ray replied. Maybe she hadn't sold it as well as she thought—sometimes it was as simple as the fact a guy was running a con meant they recognized when someone else had their own cons going on. He let it go.

"So, what's the lick?"

"Wheels," he announced.

"We're jacking a car?"

"Naw, brand new, straight off the lot," Ray answered, smiling at her confusion.

"I don't get it."

"It's simple. I've got a connect in dealership. He gave me the information for a dude who just bought a car for his precious lil princess. We're going to match the purchase, identical details, and you're going to be my lil princess," he explained.

"And what are we going to do with the car?"

"I've already got a buyer lined up."

Coco nodded.

"So, who am I? What's my name?"

"Good afternoon Mr. Taylor. Lovely to see you again. This must be your daughter," the salesman greeted Ray with a smile as slick as his handshake. They'd parked Ray's car a couple of streets away. He'd come and pick it up later.

"Dawn," Coco chimed in, flashing her pearly whites.

"Nice to meet you, Dawn. You're a lucky young lady having a dad like this." More smiles, oilier than the Exxon Valdez slick. "If you'd like to step into my office we'll get this wrapped up and have you on your way in no time," the salesman said, ushering them through to his glass-walled office.

"My name's Tom, Tom Stoyer," he introduced himself to Coco when they'd a taken a seat. "I see you like the black BMW s-series."

"I like it, but my daughter *loves* it, and try as I might, I just I can't say no to my baby," Ray said like a proud father. He patted Coco's hand affectionately.

Tom laughed.

"Same here," he admitted. "I have two girls at home, so believe me, I know *exactly* where you're coming from. Butter wouldn't melt.... Well, let me see, yes, okay, everything seems to be in order. I'm just going to need you to sign a few papers and sort the title and ownership out and then it's happy driving."

Tom slid the papers across the desk to Ray.

Ray'd been practicing the signature all week. He had the loops and flourishes down.

Coco sat back and looked around, playing the disinterested brat. Ray was good. He never left anything to chance.

"Now, your turn, Dawn."

Coco signed the papers. She'd taken a few minutes to look at the real Dawn's signature on the drive over, running a few attempts on an old envelope Ray had in the glovebox, and made a reasonable job of replicating it. It was a knack she had, and one of the reasons Ray had thought of her to play the part. She didn't need days to master a forgery.

"Okay, I'll be right back with your keys," Tom chimed, his smile as big as the commission he was counting in his mind.

As soon as he was gone, Coco laughed.

"This shit is sweet."

"You don't know the half of it. The beauty is, the card-holder will never be the wiser as long as our people keep up the payments. Hell, we even helping their credit," Ray explained. "It's a sweet sting."

They both laughed, but then cut it off abruptly when Tom walked back in.

"Congratulations, young lady. You're now the proud owner of a brand-new BMW. I think you should go buy your dad something nice to say thank you," Tom winked.

Coco snatched the dangling keys.

"South Beach here I come!" she giggled.

"Now, now, young lady, there'll be none of that," Ray mocked, in his best *Leave it to Beaver* voice.

They all laughed, but Tom had no clue the joke was really on him.

They crossed the forecourt to where the BMW was waiting, and clambered in. With a wave to a grinning Tom, they pulled out, and Coco could finally breathe a sigh of relief. She waited until they had covered a couple of blocks before she pulled off her wig.

"That was the easiest eight grand I've ever made," Coco said.

"Well not yet it ain't. We still gotta get this baby over to the buyer," Ray reminded her.

"Who is it?"

"Some older dame."

"Older?" Coco scowled, "What the fuck would a grandma want with a tagged BMW?"

The red flags in her mind went off.

Ray just shrugged.

"She ain't old-old, just like in her forties. Besides, as long as she got sixteen-grand, I don't care *who* she is. That cash spends just as well. Hells, she might even have a mark of her own to sell it on to. We all get a little richer. Money make the world go round and round, ma."

They drove for a couple of miles, then pulled into a half-empty underground garage.

"There she is," Ray pointed out, as they pulled up on a green Jaguar.

Ray parked in front of the Jag, nose-to-nose, and Coco saw the woman behind the wheel.

She could tell the woman had some age on her, but she wore it well.

Ray slid out.

The woman got out of the Jaguar, but her eyes stayed on Coco.

"Who's that?" The buyer asked, stone-faced.

"My partner. She's cool, don't sweat," Ray assured her.

The woman glared at Coco for a moment longer.

"Tell her to get out. I want her where I can see her."

"Yo, it ain't that serious," Ray chuckled.

The woman began to walk away.

"Okay, okay. Yo, ma, get out for a sec," Ray tapped on the glass.

Coco didn't like it. Her gut was telling her something wasn't right, but all she had was the razor she'd slipped into her mouth and, looking around, she figured it had to be a hundred feet to the nearest exit.

She sighed hard and clambered out of the BMW.

"Happy now?" Coco spat, rolling her eyes at the woman.

The woman looked at the car.

"So, it worked, huh?"

"Didn't I tell you it would?" Ray replied, all swagger.

"You did, you did," she nodded. "I just didn't think you could pull it off."

"Ye of little faith." Ray held out the keys. "Signed, sealed, and delivered."

"Straight to the jailhouse steps."

"Huh?" Ray guffawed.

The woman pulled out a nine-millimeter pistol and leveled it at Ray's chest.

"FBI! Don't move!"

Ray froze, but Coco bolted. The blade might be ok to use

on someone like Jose, catching him by surprise, but not against a fucking Fed with a gun. That was suicide by cop.

"One more step, and I'll blow your heart out of your goddamn chest bitch!"

Coco stopped, hands up, knowing she'd never find cover before the bullet found her.

"Both of you! On your knees. Now!"

Coco looked at Ray.

He shook his head and dropped to his knees.

The agent cuffed them both, then pushed Ray into the back seat of the Jaguar and slammed the door.

She flipped open her badge, making sure they could see it.

"Agent Vita Lewis. You're under arrest for credit card fraud."

"I ain't done nothin!" Coco protested.

Vita smiled. "Oh no? Are you sure about that? And before you lie to me, take a beat, think nice and clear, and tell me you weren't at 1051 Seymour Avenue, Apartment 211, on the afternoon of May 3rd. Then we can talk about if you 'ain't done nothin'."

Coco visibly stiffened and she felt suddenly very hot. Her heart beat faster and her legs felt leaden. She'd been looking over her shoulder since the moment she'd left Jose's apartment when she should have been looking in front of her, and now she had walked straight into a Fed's arms.

"Just as I thought."

"I don't know what you're talking about," Coco blustered.

"No? Well maybe this will refresh your memory," Vita said, ready for the denial, and held up her phone to show Coco the footage she'd scored from the jewelry store.

Coco's whole world shrunk to the size of a cell in her mind, everything closing in on her.

Vita read her expression, and a slow smile spread across her lips. She knew *exactly* what Coco was thinking.

"Now granted, this doesn't prove you killed poor old Jose, but you and I both know you did. Once I've finished matching your prints, your DNA, and the half-footprint you were stupid enough to leave in Jose's blood, I'm willing to bet a federal jury will know it too. Unlucky for you, Jose was my C.I. so I have to admit I'm taking his murder really fucking personally. And I'm going to take monumental pleasure in making sure you get that lethal injection. And I'll do it all with a smile on my face."

Coco swallowed hard.

"I want a lawyer."

"I don't give a fuck what you want. You killed a man. But I will tell you this much, you lawyer up now, you don't get to hear my deal," Vita said. "And given the huge amount of shit about to come down on your head I've got a feeling you *want* to hear what I have to say."

Coco looked at her like a drowning bitch in need of a rope.

She wasn't convinced that the woman was really about to throw her one.

But all she had left at that moment was hope.

"What deal?"

"Jose was my insider. He was working with a crew of scam artists that includes a dirty cop. He had them all lined up until you came along and fucked it up. Now I'm offering you the chance to make it right. I'd say it's the least you can do."

"How?" Coco asked, ready to join team USA. Hell, she was ready to join any team as long as it kept her on the streets.

Vita smiled because she knew it, too.

"This is your choice, you become my new C.I. You go in deep and help me put the whole lot of those scammers away, or I arrest you for fraud now, then get you convicted for murder once all those ducks are in a row. But make no mistake, you agree to this, you're mine. Body and fucking soul."

Coco shook her head fighting back the tears.

She didn't have a lot of choice.

"What do I have to do?"

"Whatever I say. But I want an answer now."

"Okay."

"Smart girl. You made the right decision," Vita told her as she handed Coco her card.

Coco read it.

"That's my office. You come by tomorrow, nine sharp. Nine oh one, I'm drawing up the arrest warrant. I'm banking on you being a smart enough bitch to know you can't run from the federal government," Vita warned. "But, just so you know, you'd better be there. Or, consequences."

Coco knew she couldn't get away.

"I won't run. What about Ray?"

"Ray's going to jail."

Vita gave Coco the key to the BMW.

"Nine sharp."

Coco looked at the key in her hand.

"I get to keep the BMW?"

"You have to look the part of a successful scammer," Vita said. "This game is all about the image. Sell the look, sell the fraud."

When Ray saw what was going down, he bellowed, "Bitch, you gonna *snitch*? Fuck, Coco! It's over for you!"

Coco looked at Vita. "What if—"

Vita cut her off. "Don't worry. We'll keep him on federal detainer until we've completed the case and they're all off the streets. It'll only be a few weeks. He won't get to sell you out."

As Coco walked to the car, she heard Ray balling, "Just wait bitch! Everybody gonna know you a rat!"

Vita looked at Coco.

"Remember, nine sharp."

Vita kept her eyes on Coco as she got into the stolen BMW and pulled away.

Coco woke the next morning, and in those first few seconds between rolling over and opening her eyes dared to hope the day before had been a nightmare. But of course it wasn't. When her new reality settled in, she took a deep breath and forced herself to get up.

She looked at herself in the mirror.

"Are you really going work for the feds? Be a rat?" She asked herself, already knowing her only answer.

It felt like she didn't have a choice.

She'd killed a rat on tape and the feds had her blood red-handed. The only way out of this shit was to dance to their beat—at least until she had enough behind her to get far, far away.

She thought of the British currency in the day bag.

An idea sprang in her head; maybe she could set up a new situation over in the U.K.? Once she was over there, new ID, new life, she was pretty sure she could move the notes. It might not be easy, but that didn't matter, it was a plan for her to aim towards once she wormed her way out from under Vita fucking Lewis and life as a C.I.. She knew how it worked, once she'd served her purpose the Feds would toss her like a piece of chewed gum.

Her first step had to be to set up contacts in the U.K.

Surely it couldn't be *that* hard if she put her mind to it?

Coco grabbed her laptop, the beginnings of a plan beginning to take shape in her mind. She set up three different profiles on social media. One for herself, then two catfish ones. One of a handsome, white dude, prime Brad Pitt white boy hot. The other a pure Nubian dark-skinned transgender female just in case she could catch someone interested.

Then she sat down and began friending random people in the U.K.

"England, here I come," she said to herself.

The first thing Coco marked as she entered Vita's office was the Federal Seal hanging on the wall, a giant reminder positioned between the American flag and the FBI flag, and in front of them, Vita's desk.

"Have a seat," the Fed instructed, without looking up from her laptop.

Coco sat down, looking around the room like she was Kyser Soze, taking it all in. She saw the picture on the wall of Vita with someone she thought could be the FBI director, though they'd gone through so many of those it could have been the one before the last one, before the one Trump booted. There was another with the governor, and one with the Agent Orange himself.

After a few moments, Vita looked up at her.

"I'm glad you made it."

"You said nine, right?"

"I know what I said, but I suspected you might try to abscond."

"Ab-what?" Coco asked.

Vita smiled. "Leave town. Attempt to elude justice. Run."

"Look, I just want to get this over with, slap the metaphorical handcuffs on and let me get on with my life," Coco shot back.

"It doesn't quite work like that. Don't get me wrong, you won't always be active. But no matter where you go, you'll always be subject to... reactivation," Vita clarified.

"So, what you're saying is like it or not I'm a snitch for life?"

"Which is better than being a prisoner for life, right?" Vita smirked. "No matter how short that life might turn out to be."

Coco shook her head. "All I want is a second chance."

"Do this right, and I'll promise to only call on you if you're needed," Vita offered, then slid a form across the desk. "It's the best I can do. You might get lucky, and we never talk to each other again. You might be unlucky and I come knocking again in six months."

Coco looked at it the paper. "What's that?"

"Informant agreement. Basically, it says you agree not to commit any other crimes, or involve yourself in nefarious behavior unless necessary for the investigation, and sanctioned by this office, and that details of the investigation are strictly confidential."

"Like, who the fuck would I tell?"

Vita shrugged. "It's just a formality. You need to cover all eventualities. It's best for both of us, so we know where we stand."

Coco skimmed over the form.

Vita held out a pen.

Coco took it, but hesitated before putting it to the paper. She looked at the other woman, expecting some sort of encouraging nod, some enticement. The woman dead-eyed her. Finally, Coco signed.

"Welcome to the team," Vita smiled, but Coco didn't smile back.

"What do I have to do?" she asked, matter-of-factly.

Vita put a picture on the desk.

Coco turned it around to face her.

The first thing that struck her was how fine he was.

"I know, I would love to fuck him, too." Vita said, reading Coco's mind. "Lucky for you, he just happens to be the mastermind behind a counterfeit credit card ring,"

"I've seen him before."

"He was Jose's connect. The guy Jose was supposed to take down. Now that's your job," Vita said.

"Okay, not to be dense, but how am I supposed to do that?"

"I've got someone else on the inside. They'll get you in. Once you're in, you'll feed intel back, take pictures, maybe even wear a wire if the time comes."

"Like Jose," Coco commented, sourly.

"Let's just hope you don't end up like him," Vita said.

"Like you care," Coco huffed.

Vita leaned forward on the desk; her hands clasped in front of her. "Okay, let's get this straight from the jump. No, I don't care if you live or die. You're scum. You murdered a man in cold blood. You're a thief and a liar. The only reason I have to care about you is that you can help me get what I want. And, between these four walls, the only reason you're not behind bars is because I cared for Jose a fuck of a lot less. So, do what I tell you, lose the attitude, and you'll get your life back."

ALEXIS

"**B**itch, I'm gonna *kill* you!"

The threat blasted through the phone so loudly Alexis had to hold the cell away from her face as she drove down the highway.

KB was full of spit and fury.

"Calm down. You ain't gonna kill nobody," Alexis giggled.

At first, she had been nervous, but Minx had schooled her how to handle KB. She'd made it all sound so easy, and maybe it would be. He might shout at her and make threats, but in the end, he wouldn't do shit about it. Not while they had their little home movie as insurance.

"You think you gonna rob me and just walk away? You know who the fuck I am?"

"Yeah," Alexis snickered, "The nigga with the dick in his ass!"

"You drugged me!"

"The fuck we did, and that's not how it looks to me in that lil movie, or how gonna look to your Instagram followers if I leak it," Alexis laughed. "They're gonna love it. Just like you did."

"When I catch you—"

"You want to talk or make idle threats? Because we both know, if something was to happen to me or my girl, not only would the video go viral, you'd be looking at a murder charge. We got contingencies in play. Oh, I'm sorry, did I mention I'm recording this call?" Alexis said.

Silence.

It lasted so long, Alexis thought he'd hung up, until he said, "What do you want?"

"Nothing," Alexis replied.

Stunned silence, though this time she was sure she could hear his breathing. His mind ticking over.

"What do you mean *nothing*?" He asked, eventually. "You gotta want something. Everyone does." His voice sounded as confused as hers had been when Minx told her the same thing.

Minx had smiled impishly in answer. *"Think about it. If we blackmail him, all we get is a few dollars. Sure, it could be damned near six figures, but we can only go to that well so many times. If we get him to follow your plan, then we're set forever. And that's so much better."*

Alexis smiled to herself.

"What kind of game you playin' bitch?" KB growled.

"First off that's the last time you call me bitch. Now, say my name," she demanded.

KB silently seethed.

"If you want this conversation to con—"

"Alexis, okay, Alexis!"

"That's better. Now, this is what you're going to do. You're going to help us lean on a few other rappers and producers.

You know who's into freaky shit they would rather be kept on the down low. You help us set up three, and we won't release your star turn," Alexis explained.

"How do I know you won't?" The was a hint of panic in his voice, but he was still talking. He could have just hung up. She had him.

"You don't, but don't have much of a choice now do you?" Alexis said, sure that he would have heard the laugh in her voice.

He thought about it for a moment, then replied, "Just three?" And sniffed.

"Just three. But they've got to be big fish you hook, and I'm giving you seven days to set it up."

"Seven? I can't—"

"You *can* and more importantly, you *will*. Byeeeee," Alexis teased, then killed the call in the face of his useless pleas.

She let out a primal *howl* as she dropped the phone on the passenger seat.

It had all gone as smooth as Minx had said it would.

Just a couple of minutes later she arrived at her destination, still feeling the exhilaration thrill through her veins.

It was super exclusive restaurant she'd asked Devante to meet her at.

It was time to close the deal.

"Beautiful," the valet said as he helped Alexis from her Porsche.

"Oh, thank you. I just bought it."

"I wasn't talking about the car," he winked, laying on the charm.

"Neither was I," she grinned, then wiggled her thick ass as she walked away from him. It always felt good to please an audience, even when they weren't paying for it.

She made her way through the tastefully crowded room filled with all those beautiful people to the table Devante occupied.

Seeing her, he stood, his face lighting up. Alexis sashayed into his embrace. A few diners glanced in their direction, but only for a moment.

"What's up gorgeous? The baby got you *glowing*," he remarked.

In your dreams, Alexis thought.

"I know," she said as Devante seated her.

Alexis picked up her glass of wine.

"White Chablis, you remembered."

"You're too beautiful to forget," he said, clearly trying to turn on the charm. "But I wondered if you should be drinking in your condition."

Before she could say how one wouldn't hurt, just to celebrate the occasion, she heard a woman's voice say, "Well isn't *this* cozy?"

Devante looked up, and his eyes damn near stretched wider than his gaping jaw.

Alexis had never seen him look like this in all the hours they'd been together.

"Monica?"

It was his wife.

"Well, at least you remembered my name, even if you forgot that we are married," Monica snapped.

"Baby, I—"

"Don't even try. The only reason I'm not spazzing is because I don't want to be on TMZ with this hood rat you dragged in. But don't push me!" Monica hissed, as she sat down, clearly seething.

For her part, Alexis had sat calmly through it all, sipping

her wine. Monica turned to her, but she was ready for anything this woman might want to throw at her.

"As much as I want to claw your face right now, I am woman enough to thank you for calling me," Monica spat.

Devante almost choked on his drink.

He couldn't believe what he was hearing.

"You *called* her?"

Alexis smirked, dangling one Louis Vuitton from her toe.

"Don't be so surprised. We're all grown-ups here, and I thought it was time we made some grown-up decisions."

"I hope you know a good divorce lawyer," Monica said, narrowing her eyes at Devante.

"Don't be silly, girl," Alexis said. "In spite of everything your man's a gold mine. He's rich, fine, and if you don't mind me sayin', got dick for days," She had to admit that she was enjoying this more than she had any right to. It felt good to see the player squirm.

"The NBA's full of guys like that," Monica returned with a raised eyebrow.

"That it is, but you know the score, they all cheaters," Alexis said, and Monica had no response for that. It was the truth. She continued, "So, you can keep your man, but you'll have to buy me out."

"Buy you out?" Monica repeated. "What you talking about, girl? This ain't no fuckin' KFC franchise we talking about."

"I'm pregnant," Alex raised her glass as she said it, the toast she'd been waiting for.

"You're what?" Monica said, her voice raising an octave. Heads turned in her direction.

"Remember TMZ," Alexis reminded her.

Monica looked around.

A few pairs of eyes on her turned away.

"You piece of *shit*," Monica spat at Devante.

"To his credit, if you can call it that, he wants me to get rid of it. Isn't that right, Devante?"

Devante shot Alexis daggers.

She smiled them away.

"So, this is my offer, my only offer, non-negotiable. Five hundred thousand."

"Five hundred?" Devante rasped.

"Take it or leave it. Because if I don't get it, then I'll keep the little bastard. You know what that means? Child support, and we both know how much that will be times eighteen years. On top of that, the media hype and yes, Monica, your precious TMZ scandal rag. Am I painting a clear enough picture?"

Devante boiled and Monica brewed.

Alexis just beamed.

She looked at her watch.

"I do have a spa appointment, people. So, do we have us a deal?"

"Pay her," Monica gritted.

"Are you *crazy*?"

"Only for not killing you. Now pay the bitch, and get her out of our lives," Monica demanded. "I never want to see or hear of her again. You understand?"

Devante glared at first one woman and then the other.

"Threats, Devante? Do you really want to go there?" Alexis said.

Devante relented. "Where do you want the money sent?"

Alexis smiled and slid him her banking information.

JORDAN

"I'm surprised."

"Because I called?"

"Because you *came*," David smiled, as he and Jordan meandered through the park.

It was a lovely evening.

They'd just finished dinner and were simply taking the time to enjoy each other's company.

"Hey, I never turn down a free meal," Jordan joked.

It had been a nice restaurant. Nothing fancy, but the food was pretty good, and the waiter hadn't been over attentive. No letching or leering.

"You're a big girl. I'm pretty sure you can take care of yourself."

Jordan shrugged.

"You just...seem like a nice guy. Not judgmental."

"Of?"

"Me. My life." She filled in the blanks. "The stripping, I guess. Most people are," she said. "Especially men."

"Well, to meet a woman in a strip club, means you have to

be in the club too, right? So, let's be honest, who am I to judge? Besides, I really admire strippers."

Jordan looked at him.

"You do? Why?"

"It takes a lot to work that pole!"

She laughed.

"Please tell me you've tried."

"No, but I mean... you can tell. It's a full-body workout. I mean, I'm a pretty fit guy, I know what kind of muscle control it takes."

Jordan looked at his toned frame and pictured him naked.

It was hard not to.

"Pretty fit is an understatement."

"Thanks."

They walked in silence for a moment, until Jordan said, "Can I ask you something?"

"Sure."

"What made you want to be a cop?" She wasn't sure why she asked, but she'd never been with one out of choice before.

At least as far as she knew.

That was a strange thought to have... not knowing her own past.

David seemed to struggle for a moment then replied, "In a way, I guess the easiest way to explain it is that it felt like what was expected of me. My grandfather was a cop, my father was a cop, and when I came home from the marines—" That was all Jordan heard before her mind was flooded with the sounds of gunfire and military barks.

"Move! Move! Move!"

Screams of pain, the smell of death in the air, and lights flashing in her eyes.

"Jordan?" David's voice cut through the sounds of the

flashback, snapping her back to reality. Her heart was beating like a galloping horse in her chest.

"Are you okay?" He asked, his hands on her shoulders, bracing her as she slowly dissolved out of the past.

"Just need to... sit down."

He nodded.

They found a nearby bench and sat.

Ever the gentleman, David slipped off his jacket and wrapped it around her shoulders.

"Thank you," Jordan said, not even realizing she'd been shivering until the comfort of David's gesture made her stop.

"What happened back there? I mean one minute you were fine, and the next you just stopped walking and began mumbling in some other language," he told her.

Jordan looked at him.

"Another language?"

"Yeah. I don't know what it was, but I said your name like ten times before you even reacted," David said, shaking his head. "That, I don't mind admitting, was pretty fucking frightening."

Jordan saw the way he was looking at her. *He must think I'm crazy,* she thought shamefully.

"I don't know what happened. I just heard all of these... these... noises, screams, and gunshots. It was—" Jordan shrugged. She couldn't even finish the sentence. Her voice gave way to sobs that she couldn't control.

David wrapped an arm around her and held her tight.

"It's okay, Jordan. You're good," he said. "I've got you."

When her sobs finally subsided, he asked her, "Do you speak any other languages?"

Jordan thought hard then shook her head.

"I don't know."

"You don't know?"

Jordan took a deep breath then decided she needed to hell him. "I was some kind of traffic accident. The driver died, but I still don't know who he was. I-I...I don't even know who I am."

"Wow," David said, shaking his head.

"Please don't think I'm crazy," she said.

"No, it's not that," he smiled reassuringly. "It's your accent. It's changed since you had that blackout."

"Changed?"

"It's like... I don't know how to explain it... You sound like someone who's second language is English now," he said.

Jordan couldn't hear it herself.

"You sound sort of like this guy who works in a restaurant down the block from here. Matter of fact..."

He grabbed Jordan's hand and they got up.

"Where are we going?"

"To find your tribe."

Jordan and David walked into the small restaurant; the smell of curried goat filled the space.

The smell seemed incredibly familiar to her.

It made Jordan feel relaxed, comforted.

David stepped to the counter where an older black man with steel gray hair and a few teeth was kneading dough.

"Ah my man, him back," the old man cackled.

David smiled.

"What's up Joseph? I've got someone I want you to meet."

Joseph looked at Jordan and smiled a wide, near toothless grin.

"The old man always ready to meet dem young gal," he said.

David chuckled, then turned to Jordan.

"Go ahead, introduce yourself," David urged.

"Hello, I'm Jordan. I'm a friend of David."

Joseph's face lit up.

"Ah my man, you didn't tell me her Haitian," he remarked, then began to speak to her in Creole.

Jordan couldn't believe her ears. She understood *every* word. Unfortunately, her tongue couldn't provide a proper response.

"You can understand, but not speak?" Joseph asked her, still in Creole.

"I'm sorry. It... it's been a while," she said.

"Well keep coming to see ol' Joseph," he laughed. "I'll have you better in no time!"

She laughed until tears streamed down her face.

"Are you okay?" David asked.

"Never better," she said, because they were tears of joy, of a light in the tunnel.

She felt like maybe, just maybe, she had found a piece of herself.

David walked her to the door of her room.

When she entered, he didn't follow her inside.

"I, uh, had a wonderful evening," David said, awkwardly.

Jordan stood just inside the room, the darkness and the hint of moonlight accentuating her soft smile.

"Aren't you going to kiss me goodnight?"

David smiled and stepped inside.

"Your wish is my command."

He stepped inside and pulled Jordan into his arms, pressing his lips against hers and sliding his tongue into her mouth. She gripped his back and he palmed her ass, as she moaned into his mouth, giving herself over to the kiss.

He pulled her skirt down then lay her in the bed.

"Damn, you beautiful." he whispered.

He ran his tongue up the softness of her thigh until he reached her clit.

The first lick sent a shiver through her that turned into a tremor.

"Oh God," she gushed, spreading her legs, and arching her back.

David cradled her ass cheeks in his hands then feasted on her sweetness.

"My turn," Minx cooed, coming out of the shadows where she had been waiting, hidden. Jordan hadn't even realized she was there, but didn't object to sharing the man with her. A promise was a promise.

Minx laughed.

Jordan swooned.

David thought he was in love.

"So, this was when you first discovered your ethnicity?" Myers asked.

"Yes," Jordan answered.

"Haitian?"

"I am."

Myers nodded, letting that settle in. He turned to scan the jury's faces one by one, making sure they appreciated the implications of that revelation before he asked, "And it has helped you remember other things about your past?"

Jordan took a deep breath.

"I...I was a sex slave... in Haiti. They took in children and young women, but they...they sold us to wealthy Americans. We were located by the US marines and liberated. A lot of it's still confused. Guess my head is still trying to work it all out. "

"I can't even begin to imagine what you've been through. You have my deepest sympathies, and, I'm sure those of everyone in this court. Do you mind explaining, is this how you came to America?" Myers asked.

Jordan hesitated. Shrugged.

"I don't know."

"Let me help you. It's listed in the official reports that you arrived thanks to help from your soon-to-be husband, Victor. Do you remember that?"

"No."

"If it pleases the court, I'd like to show the witness exhibit 17, a photograph."

"Very good," the judge acceded, gesturing for the DA to bring the photograph forward.

She studied it.

The man in the photograph looked well built, strong, confidant.

She frowned and pushed the picture away.

"No."

"Are you sure?"

Jordan glared.

"I said no!"

Myers said, "For the record, I'm showing the witness a photograph of two people, herself, and a tall brown skinned man with curly hair. Victor." He turned back to her. "Now, remember you are under oath. I have another question. Detective Wingate?"

"What about him?"

"In your statement you said that you slept with him?"

"Yes." She hadn't given him all the details, but she had told him everything he needed to know.

"Both you and... Minx?"

Again, the knowing smirk.

"Yes."

"Did you know who he was when you slept with him?" Myers probed.

"You mean, did I know he was a detective?"

"No, did you know who he really was...?"

COCO

Vita didn't waste any time getting Coco into the mix.

She didn't really know anything about her new C.I., but Vita sent her to meet two dudes, she called them Cory and Flacco, at a nearby IHOP. She'd never understood people who went to a pancake place and didn't order pancakes. It was in the name.

Flacco was Dominican and black.

Corey was heavy set. Not exactly fat, sure as hell not thin.

Coco walked in and was about to sit down when they both stood up, left a tip, and started for the door.

"You missed breakfast," Flacco spat disgustingly over his shoulder.

"Whatever," Coco mumbled, already loathing her two accomplices. She followed them out to their waiting wheels.

They got in the car, with Coco in the back, and pulled off, music pumping.

She kept a close eye on Corey, the driver, as he slipped the car onto the highway.

"Where we going?" Coco asked. Vita hadn't told her

anything beyond the fact she was meant to meet these two guys, and she'd arrived bang on the time she had been given. It felt like they intended to give the new girl a hard time, which wasn't great but she'd play the game.

"You'll see when we get there," Corey replied, then turned up the music to drown out any more questions.

Coco sat in the back, fuming.

She was ready to bail, but kept reminding herself what was at stake. Play the game or face serious time. She stifled her anger, sat back, and tried to enjoy the ride.

A few hours later, they reached the suburban outskirts of a city.

"Ay yo, sleeping beauty. Time to earn your keep," Flacco said, waking Coco up.

She roused herself and took a moment to look around. She saw the city limits sign. Wilmington, Delaware. The traffic around them was all moving at the same speed and there was plenty of it.

"Where are we?" she asked, because it was the natural question for her to ask.

"That don't matter," Flacco snapped back. "You just here to do a job, and it don't matter where we're doing it. All you have to do, sister, is what we tell you."

"Hold up. First of all, you don't know me 'kay? Second, you don't want to know me, but if you keep poppin' slick, we gonna get introduced real quick," Coco sassed.

Flacco looked at Corey and smiled.

"My bad, shorty."

"Coco. Not shorty."

Corey and Flacco exploded into laughter and that was enough to break the ice.

"My bad, Coco. It's just we see so many chicks come and

go, none of them last. We keep our distance," Flacco explained. "Easier than bein' friends."

"Still, that ain't no reason for that pissy assed attitude," she said.

"You're right, Coco. My bad. How 'bout we be friends now?" Flacco smiled and his dimples made her smile back.

"I can't be friends with people whose name I don't know."

"I'm Flacco, this is Corey."

"Why do they call you Flacco? Don't that mean skinny in Spanish?" she said, because he was far from skinny. He had the physique of a boxer.

"I was a li'l nigga back in the day, and it stuck," he replied. "Didn't matter what I ate, I never put on any weight. And when your family don't have a lotta cash, there's not much opportunity to each *too* much. Flacco was nowhere near as bad as some of the shit they called me. I started workin' out and got bigger. Time came those kids who called me names stopped. Or I stopped them."

"And you still call yourself Flacco?"

"Call it a reminder," he said. "Sometimes you have to hang onto some of the bad stuff to remind yourself of who you are and where you come from."

"Yeah," she agreed.

"So, can we get this bag, or do you want to know my whole life story?" Flacco smirked.

Coco playfully mushed his head.

"There goes that shitty attitude," she laughed.

Corey handed her the check.

She eyed it. It was for $50,000.

"We stayed up most of the night printing these damned things," he chuckled, then followed the check up with a driving license that had her photo on it, and the name, Janice Freeman.

"Nice job," she approved.

"It's the only way it will work," Flacco said and she knew he was right, as long as the check was good enough to get paid out on. It could take weeks for a bad check to get spotted if the account holder had big enough balance, and she assumed that someone had done their research.

"You ready?" Corey asked.

"No doubt about it," Coco assured him.

They pulled into the parking lot of the bank, parked, and turned off the engine.

"Let me see if you 'bout this business," Flacco teased.

"Watch me work," she winked, then got out.

She wore a conservative pant suit, but she could feel Flacco and Corey's eyes on her ass. She teased them with a little stank in her walk. She'd bet the other girls they'd worked with hadn't given them the same good treat.

"Damn," she heard Flacco say through the open car window, stretching it out appreciatively, before she disappeared into the bank.

Inside, she moved with confidence as she stepped into line. Part of the scam was looking like you belonged. The bank was moderately busy, and taking a look around she realized almost all of the customers were white. *Stupid motherfuckas. Why you go to a white bank where I'll stand out?* Coco's mind huffed as she silently cursed out her co-conspirators. They couldn't have made her more memorable if they'd tried.

She marked the white security guard looking at her.

For a split-second she was nervous, that ripple of fear that he somehow knew what was going on, then she realized he was looking at her ass. When he saw that he was busted, he gave her a sheepish grin, shrugged and quickly looked away.

Coco stepped to the counter.

"Good morning, welcome to Unified Banking," the blond teller greeted, a faker than fake smile plastered on a face that had too much make-up.

Coco slid the check to her.

"Yes, I'd like to cash this."

"No problem, madam. I'll need to see your ID."

"Of course."

Coco handed her the fake driving license.

The teller looked at it then remarked, "Oh, Ms. Green. I see you're from New York?"

Coco cursed under her breath, wondering why the guys in the car hadn't thought to give her a driving license with a local address. It was like they were deliberately trying to get her busted.

"I'm in the process of moving here. Haven't had time to get it updated. Planning a wedding is hell," Coco covered, spotting the wedding band on the teller's finger and playing the solidarity card.

"Tell me about it," she replied, handing Coco the money in a bank envelope, "Welcome to Wilmington."

"Thank you," Coco replied, taking the cash.

She didn't show a lick of emotion until she was out the door, but as soon as she hit the car, she let free with a stream of invective aimed at her two new 'friends'.

"Whose bright fucking idea was it to go all the way to Wilmington?" she spat.

"The local banks were getting hot," Corey responded.

"Well, goddamn, I wish you would've told me! The bitch asked about my out-of-town ID."

Corey glanced in the rearview mirror as he drove out of the lot.

"You didn't have any problems, did you?"

"I didn't come out running, did I? Next time give me a heads up, that's all I'm saying," Coco grouched as she handed Corey and Flacco their cut.

The rest of the day went smoothly.

They hit up eight more banks, a check printed ready for each one, and racked up $500,000 before calling it a very decent days grift.

"Damn, my feet are killin' me," Coco said, taking off her stiletto boots and savoring the sudden relief.

She massaged her toes to relieve the ache.

"Should've worn flats," Flacco said. "Shit, what if you had to run?"

"Believe me, a sister knows how to rock out these heels and get lost," she laughed. "You'll be surprised how fast I can hustle if I really have to." Then she remembered her getaway in the mall. At least then she had been able to kick them off as she ran. It wouldn't have been so easy in these boots.

"I'm hungry as hell," Corey said, slowing down as taillights ahead glowed red.

"Let's hit up Applebee's," Coco suggested, spotting a familiar sign a little way along the street. If they were IHOP boys they were probably Applebee's boys. A couple of minutes later they have found somewhere to park and headed inside.

Sitting at the table, the three of them bantered back and forth.

It was good. Natural. She fit into their world.

Flacco sat across from her, giving Coco a chance to really drink in his swag.

Damn, he kinda fine, she thought to herself, feeling that familiar twitch.

She knew one of them was working for Vita as a C.I., just like her, but she didn't know which one. She figured she could find out. She'd just have to play them off one another and gain her own kind of informant.

Nothing beats a cross, but a double cross, she thought to herself.

"So Flacco, you got a girlfriend?" She asked while Corey had left them alone to pay a call to the bathroom.

Flacco smiled and sipped his drink. "Yeah."

"Too bad...for her," Coco smiled.

Flacco laughed. "So, why do you ask?"

"I just wanted to know what kind of situation I'm getting into," she said.

"What kind of a situation you *trying* to get into?" He corrected for her.

Her look said it all.

"Damn ma. You don't play no games, huh?"

"When I see what I want, I don't hesitate. I just go out and get it," she replied, wrapping her lips seductively around the straw in her drink.

"Hold that thought," Flacco chuckled as Corey came back to the table.

Flacco looked at his watch.

"Ya'll tryin' to hit the road or what?"

"Shit. I'm tired as fuck, and those backseat naps are not hittin' it," Coco chimed in.

"Fuck it," Corey said. "Why don't we just get some rooms

and roll out in the morning," Corey said. They didn't take a lot of convincing.

They drove to a nearby hotel and checked in.

Corey used his fake ID and a scammed card to pay for three rooms. Corey and Flacco had adjoining rooms while Coco had one across the hall, One that she didn't plan on staying in long.

She took a shower, then got down with the hotel's complimentary lotion. When she'd finished, she didn't even bother to get dressed. She simply threw on the terry cloth robe she found hanging on the back of the bathroom door, and crossed the hall to deliver her gift.

She knocked on the door.

It didn't take Flacco long to answer.

"Knock, knock," she said seductively, when Flacco opened the door and stepped inside without waiting to be invited.

She let the robe slip open to giving him a look at the goods on offer.

He locked the door and when he turned back the robe hit the floor. Her body was beautiful, her breasts ripe, and her stomach cut. Flacco licked his lips like it was dinner time.

"See something you like?" Coco purred.

Flacco took her around the waist and tongued her down like he was trying to lick all the way into her tonsils. He squeezed her soft ass, spreading and massaging her cheeks.

"Damn this ass soft," he grinned.

"So, what are you going to do with it?" she whispered.

"Bend over," Flacco demanded.

"You gonna fuck me rough, baby? I love it rough," Coco said.

She was so loud she didn't hear the door of Corey's adjoining room open up and Corey enter, watching the show.

"Goddamn homie, break bread," Corey swore, watching Coco's ass swing and wobble like Jell-o.

Corey approached Coco.

She was in a zone, panting, too far gone to say no even if she had wanted to. She was in that place where she was open to anything and Corey had no problem obliging.

Back in her room, she saw she had three missed calls from Vita.

Coco called back.

"Everything go as planned?" Vita asked, not bothering with niceties like saying hello.

"As well as can be expected. I ain't in jail," Coco said breezily.

"Did you make contact with the mastermind yet?"

"It's only my first day."

"It could be your last one free if you don't lose that attitude. Bottom line is results. That's your situation. If you don't get any, then what good are you to me?" Vita shot back.

Coco took a deep breath.

"I'll produce."

"That's more like it. Now, how many banks did you hit today? Remember, don't lie."

"Nine banks," Coco answered.

"How much did you make?"

"500,000 dollars."

"Okay. Save every dime of your cut. When we meet, you'll turn it in, every dollar will be logged and then we will both sign for it," Vita explained.

"What about me? I still have bills to pay," Coco complained.

"You'll receive a stipend. I can't let you keep any of the proceeds from your criminal activities, that's not how this works, but I'll make sure you are taken care of, you have my word," Vita promised.

Coco shook her head.

What the fuck have I gotten myself into? She thought sourly.

JORDAN

"So, why aren't you married and tucked away in a mansion somewhere living a life of luxury?" David joked, as he and Jordan strolled along the street, taking in the night air and the sights and smells of Chinatown.

Across the street a crag-faced woman with a licorice paper wrapped cigarillo sucked on the end and puffed smoke as she washed down the tenement stoop. The next door along another woman cut from the same mold chopped cabbage on a wooden board balanced across her knees.

"Well, first off, because the right man hasn't asked me, I suppose. And second, I don't think I'm the kinda girl who gets tucked away anywhere," Jordan replied, with a playful sass in her voice.

David held his hands up in mock surrender.

"My bad, Miss Diva. Well, if I can't tuck you away, can I at least tuck you in?" He flirted.

Jordan blushed.

"Sound pretty sure of yourself, Mr. Policeman."

David shrugged.

"Believe me, this badge doesn't define me."

"Then what does?"

David thought for a minute, then replied, "My sense of humor. My capacity to love, and forgive, and most of all, the strength of my character."

Jordan pursed her lip, impressed.

"So, then the question is, why aren't you married?"

They laughed.

As they drove home, Jordan massaged the back of his neck from the passenger seat.

"That feels good," he said, savoring her touch.

"Oh yeah?" Jordan said. "I know something that would feel even better," She gave a playful smile then lowered her head towards his crotch.

It was then that David saw the gun. If she hadn't bent down at the precise moment, her brains would've been in his lap for a whole different reason.

"Oh *shit*," David gasped.

Skreeeechh!

Boc! Boc!

He pulled away just in time, Jordan screaming.

"What's going on?"

She could feel the panic in her voice, matching the sudden increase in her heartbeat.

Something was way wrong.

"Stay down."

There were three gunmen, including the driver, in hot pursuit.

Boc!

Boosh!

The back window shattered, exploding inwards in a shower of

glass. Some sliced at Jordan's face. The temptation was to scream some more, but she kept it inside. David ducked and swerved. The car fishtailed. More shots. David pulled on his cellphone.

"Officer in need of assistance, shots fired, I repeat, officer in need of assistance, shots fired," he screamed as he pulled out his gun.

"Who is this? Identify yourself, officer," dispatch questioned.

"Detective Wingate. Badge Number 9371. I'm in the city! Triangulate the call!" He demanded, then dropped the phone, leaving the call open.

He turned to Jordan.

"Grab the wheel!"

She did.

"Hold it steady while we switch," David ordered her, simultaneously lifting her up and over as he scooted under, until he was in the passenger seat.

Boc! Boc! Boc!

The shots were coming hot and heavy, breaking more glass, and dinging off metal in a brutal ricochet symphony.

"Make this next right, then slow down. I'm going to jump out. Count to five then stop. You got it?" David instructed.

Jordan nodded furiously.

She took the next right then slowed.

David dove out, curling his body into the perfect roll as he hit the blacktop. He was banking on the fact that when the gunmen came around the corner, they wouldn't make him where he was crouched in the shadows.

Jordan stopped the car.

The gunmen stopped several feet back and waited for a moment. They should've just hopped out and ran up to the car, that was the smart play. But seeing his car stop must have thrown them off their game.

They smelled a trap.

And they were about to stroll right up into it.

A faked out muscle and oil dude jumped out of the back seat of car, calling back to the driver, "I don't give a *fuck*. I'm getting' paid to do a job and Ima doing it."

Boc! Boc!

Two shots exploded his melon from behind, blowing brain and blood all over the door.

"Oh shit! Oh sh—" was all the driver got out before the next bullet exploded through his throat.

David rushed up to the car in time to watch him choking on his own blood before he died.

David aimed his gun at the last gunman, scrunched down in the passenger seat.

"Don't shoot! Please!" Dropping his gun, he held his hands up, palms out, pleading.

David couldn't see his face in the shadows, but when he shifted his weight, the moonlight illuminated his features.

"Damn!" David gasped.

Jordan heard the sirens and prayed a silent prayer of relief.

She waited in the car, her hands still gripping the steering wheel, her heartbeat finally starting to slow as her breathing came under control.

In the distance she heard the sound of sirens racing to get to them.

"You know you're in so deep in the shit right now you're drowning, right? Trying to kill a cop? It's over you stupid, stupid, boy," David hissed in the young gunman's face.

They were in the interrogation room, along with another detective.

The young thug tried to play tough, but the dried tears cracked on his cheeks betrayed him. He'd cried all the way to the stationhouse, and on through the fifteen minutes they had made him stew.

"I want my lawyer," he stammered, deepening his voice, like it could make up for the fact he'd cried like a girl.

"You think you can lawyer up after you tried to kill me?" David shook his head. "You get that that's unforgivable, right? I'll tell you what, lawyer up. Just wait 'til you get upstate. I got a few dudes that would *love* to earn themselves probation by doing me a favor," David said, the threat more than just implicit.

He pushed the chair back, rose and headed for the door.

David knew that the young gunman would have heard all the stories about the county jail. No banger in their right mind wanted to end up there willingly, especially not with a target painted on his back. He did what David always knew he would.

"Man, okay," he blurted out.

David stopped, waited a beat, hand on the door then turned to look at him.

"Okay, *what*?"

"I'll tell you whatever you want to know," the young banger answered, his head hung with shame, like he was breaking omerta, and plenty of fear in that downward glance. His feet weren't that interesting.

David concealed his smirk, but nodded to the other detective in the interrogation room. He sat back down.

"I'm listening."

"We didn't know there was a cop in the car. You got to believe me."

"What do you mean, didn't know?" David probed.

The young gunman shrugged.

"The hit ain't have nothing to do with you."

"Hit?"

"Yeah. What you think it was?"

"I'd assumed a fucked-up carjacking," David replied.

The young gunman laughed.

"Naw, dawg, that was a hit. Plain and simple. We were sent to kill the bitch."

"Watch your mouth, kid. Okay, you've got me intrigued. Who put out the hit?"

The young man shifted in his seat.

"Talk now or bleed later," David growled.

"Come on man, I just said it ain't have nothing to do with you. That nigga will kill me if I say—"

David sighed theatrically, and pushed the legs of his chair back. "Go tell receiving to put him in D-pod," the other detective nodded. But before he could move, the young boy blurted out, "Cool V! Cool V put the hit on her!"

David looked at him.

"Let me get this straight, you're saying *The* Cool V?"

"You know another one?"

David knew then, he had his hands full.

"And then they just started shooting," Jordan exclaimed, shaking her head.

"Fuck girl, that's crazy fucked up," Minx remarked.

"I mean, first I'm with you and they start shooting at you. Then I'm with David, and they start shooting at him?" She shook her head. "What the hell is going on?"

Minx smirked.

"Ever think maybe they're shooting at you?"

"Me? For what?" She hadn't even considered the possibility she could be the target. Why would she? She was no one.

Before Minx could respond, Jordan's phone rang.

She answered.

David. "I'm downstairs. We have to talk," he said, his voice hard and unyielding.

"I was just about—"

"Now, Jordan."

Jordan put on her shoes and headed for the door.

"How do you know Cool V, and why would he want you dead?" David asked, voice knife-sharp, eyes sharper. Jordan hadn't even closed the car door.

"Cool V? I don't know any Cool V," she replied, honestly. She tried to think, hoping that the name might ring a bell, but it brought back *nothing*.

"Don't lie to me, Jordan."

"I swear!"

"So why would he send a hit team after you?" David demanded.

"You mean those people were after me?"

Jordan shook her head. It made no sense. And yet she could just imagine Minx saying, "I told you."

"Yeah. The one surviving suspect confirmed it. He said it was a hit ordered by Cool V They were after *you*. So, what aren't you telling me?"

Jordan shook her head.

"I told you about my accident, and the guy that died. Maybe it has something to do with that? I don't know. It's making my brain hurt..." Jordan told him, massaging her temples against the sting of pain trying to remember brought with it.

Seeing her vulnerable and distressed was enough to make David take a deep breath. He looked around. He was parked in front of her building, and she was the target. The obvious move from Cool V's side was to put eyes on the block. David needed to stay on point. He couldn't let his guard slip, even for a moment.

"Okay, look. The first thing I have to do is find out who the guy with you was, see if that makes a difference, or if it is really you they want and no amount of amnesia will buy your life."

"You're scaring me, David."

"You should be scared. These are serious people."

"Can I ask you something, David? Don't think I'm being stupid or clever... Who is Cool V?"

"He's the kingpin. Runs the entire East coast. If there's a pie he's got his finger in it. He owns got cops, judges, politicians, hell, even preachers, in his pocket. He might as well be Jesus. He rules his streets with an lead," David explained, leaving no room for misunderstanding.

"Oh my God... I'm sorry... I should never have gotten you involved in this... with me... But I have no idea what's going on. Maybe we shouldn't see each other anymore..." Jordan sobbed, her voice trailing off in tears. "Maybe I should get away while I can. Run. The further, the better."

David had already run that scenario through his mind.

He'd thought about walking away and leaving her alone, too.

But the truth was he couldn't face that because he was already falling for her. It might not be love yet, but it would be. He was in no doubt about that. There was something growing here. Seeds. He took a deep breath and replied, "No. I'm not going to abandon you. We'll get through this together."

He took her hand and gave it a comforting squeeze.

"Thank you."

He leaned over and kissed her. It wasn't passionate, it was reassuring. It said, right now, I'm your best hope.

"But there is somebody I need you to meet. She's a federal agent."

"A federal agent?"

"Yeah. If we're going to protect you from Cool V, we'll need all the help we can enlist."

"Who is she?"

"She's FBI. Agent Vita Lewis."

He knew it was already a bad day before he looked up the deceased from Jordan's accident. The second that face come up on the screen that bad day turned a fuck of a lot worse. He recognized Spaz immediately despite the postmortem photograph and the damage from the crash. He'd never forget *that* face.

"Damn baby, what the fuck is going on?" He mumbled to himself, shaking his head. This was some serious bad shit unfolding. He pulled out his phone and dialed. After two rings, Vita answered.

"Yeah," she said.

"I need your help, V."

"Just call me Obi-fuckin'-Wan, Princess."

He didn't laugh.

VITA

"I'll call you as soon as I get back to the office," she promised said then hung up.

"Booty call?" Alexis teased, as she sucked seductively on the flavored straw in her drink.

Vita smirked.

"Something like that. Now, what were you saying?"

Alexis put down her drink.

"I'm thinking about getting into the music biz," she said, with a mischievous smirk.

"Oh? And what brought this exciting change of career on?" Vita asked.

Alexis toyed with her straw, eyes sweeping the club's interior. She watched the dancers getting their money as Baller's parted company with dead presidents. They were having to work hard for it and pickings were pretty slim.

"Let's just say, I've got KB Ballin by the balls. Literally."

Vita leaned in, interest piqued. Ballin was a big name; a real mover and shaker.

"Do tell."

Alexis pulled out her phone and showed Alexis the pictures of KB and the dildo.

After the initial moment of shock, Vita grinned, and that grin turned into a proper belly laugh. She'd never seen anything quite like it. A couple of the girls looked in their directions but the customers only had eyes for the goods on the stage.

"Bitch, you have him for real. How much is he paying you to keep the little indiscretion hush hush?"

"Nothing," Alexis shrugged.

"Nothing?" Vita echoed. "I don't follow. Talk me through it."

"If I ask him for money, then that would be extortion and blackmail."

"True. And you've suddenly become all law-abiding, or are you asking my permission to turn blackmailer?"

"Naw, thinking bigger. If he's as big a bitch as the dildo makes him look, he could get the police involved."

"He could, but I can't imagine he would. Not in his world. It's all about face and he'd lose it all if that little home movie went public."

"That's my thinking too. But if I get him to help us set up other celebs, we can use them to open doors to real money," Alexis explained.

Vita thought about it, then nodded.

"That's the smart play. You're an evil genius, kid," Vita said in appreciation.

"I know," Alexis said, not letting on that it was Minx who'd cooked up the scheme.

"So, you get him to do your beats and while he's at it, use his celeb status to get the dirt on other names and use the same dildo up the ass against them?" Vita asked.

"You?"

"All I gotta do is look good, and let Pro Tools do their thing," Alexis purred, striking a pose.

"I gotta admit, it's not the worst plan I've ever heard," Vita said, but thinking she might have a better one.

"Can I tell KB what this about?" asked the receptionist at the front desk.

Vita showed the receptionist her badge.

"Federal inquiry. Voluntary, but necessary."

The receptionist looked nodded, concealing any shock behind a mask of professionalism. She picked up the phone. Vita took a moment to look around the spacious office of Ballin Records. KB Ballin had a rep for doing things big in the industry. The offices fronted an even bigger ego. But there was a reason behind the ego; his label was one of the top in the game.

Now, if Vita could turn him...Then she'd make *her* name.

"KB says he'll see you."

"Thank you."

"It's the office at the end of the hall. You can't miss it."

Vita walked along the plush carpet to the gold-plated double doors at the end of the hallway.

Money can't buy you taste, I guess, she thought to herself, but reasoned that it made for a good façade. She could imagine that plenty of people fronting up to these doors *would* be impressed. It was like Trump's golden elevators. Anyone who came from nothing couldn't help but want a piece of this Midas shit, and beyond those doors was just the man to touch their shit and turn it to cold hard cash.

She took a breath then knocked.

"Come in."

KB sat behind a large desk, the skyline spread out behind him through a wall of glass. It was far more impressive than the fake glitz and gold.

"My secretary said this shit is voluntary," KB said.

"It is, absolutely, but necessary," Vita assured him.

"Okay, well, just so we're clear, the minute I feel it's no longer voluntary, this little tête a tête will be concluded," he replied.

"Fair enough."

He invited her to sit in one of the chairs opposite him.

"So, what do you think I can I do for you?"

"I'd like your thoughts on this," Vita said, as she slid her phone across the desk. The incriminating video was already playing. She'd cloned Alexis's phone before she turfed her loose to play CI. She'd already seen the movie when the girl had shown it to her.

He took one look at the screen and didn't need to see more. His eyes dilated with recognition, but he shoved it back with a gruff, "That's not me."

"Sure looks like you."

"Like I said—" His face was already looking flushed, a sheen of sweat glistening on his forehead.

"You know where I got this video, I'm sure."

No response.

"You don't *have* to answer, just listen. I know Alexis is using this video as leverage to force you into compromising other clients and friends," Vita said.

"I don't know what you're talking—"

"Don't bother lying," Vita raised a hand to silence him. He didn't seem to be used to people treating him like that. His eyes burned. "I know it's you, you know it's you and I wanted remind you know, blackmail is a federal crime. So, the thing is, now that I am aware of the situation I cannot in good faith allow this to go on."

"What are you going to do?"

"First, I'm going to arrest Alexis. Then there will be a trial, and of course, during the trail the video will be a key piece of evidence."

"Key? As in it will be *out* there? You can't do that shit, that's criminal," KB blurted out, his face turning a shade darker.

KB sighed.

"Look, please, you can't put this out there. If you do, I'm ruined." He held his arms out expansively as if to display the size of his empire. "All this will all disappear overnight."

He looked like he might be ready to kill himself, maybe even do a *Hudsucker Proxy* and climb up onto the table and run, hurling himself out himself out of the window behind him. Breaking point reached, zero real pressure applied. The guy was all front.

"So, you'd rather let Alexis use you and coerce you into committing federal crimes that admit to any sexual deviance?"

"What choice do I have?"

"Well, there is one."

"What?"

"One shot deal. Become my Confidential Informant."

He frowned, everything about the two words setting off a war of guilt, fear and hate in his gut. "You want me to become a snitch?"

"I'd prefer to call it a C.I. You won't actually be sending anyone to jail, and you won't be expected to testify against anyone. Your rep will be clean. No one will have a clue. If it helps your conscience, think of it as us becoming friends, all I need my new friend to do is keep me abreast of Alexis's requests, give me an idea of what dirt you dig up on who, and fill me in," Vita explained.

"How's that going to help me?"

"Quid pro Quo, Clarice," she said, smiling as dead-eyed as Hannibal Lector ever did. "Once I've what I need on her, the clip will be buried forever. You have my word. It will never see the light of day," Vita vowed.

"And that crazy bitch won't know?" KB asked.

Vita shook her head.

"She doesn't know I'm an agent. She just thinks I like pussy."

"Do you?" he cracked, forgetting the shit he was in for just a second.

Vita chuckled and stood up, extending her card to him.

"Here's my number. I'll expect to hear from you. If I don't, and I find out Alexis has... Well, you know the rest."

Vita walked out, knowing she had KB in her pocket, and he was staying there.

"He... He was good to me," Jordan said, fighting back tears.

"But he lied to you about who he was," Myers reminded her, making sure the court knew exactly what he meant. "That has to sting. Especially given everything you've told us about your unique situation."

Jordan leveled her eyes on him.

"We all lie," she said.

"That is true, of course. And some lies cost us our lives."

"And some cost us other people's lives," Jordan shot right back, and regretted it instantly.

He had her rattled.

Myers sighed and cleaned his glasses.

She was starting to wonder if it was something he did to buy him time think or to emphasize a point. It was a play. That much she knew. He was fronting, just like the lowest corner boy.

"I don't want to argue with you."

"We're not arguing," he said.

"I'm only here because I agreed to help."

"I know, and I appreciate that. We all do. We're all here for the same reason, to establish the truth. And we know we can't get anywhere unless you're willing to tell us the truth. I'd like to remind you of the oath you swore when you took the stand."

"I've been nothing but truthful."

Myers shook his head.

"I don't think that's entirely accurate."

"Why?"

"Because I know you haven't told me the truth about Minx..."

Minx walked through the front door of the church. She couldn't help but snicker to herself.

"At least I didn't burst into flames."

It had been a while since she last set foot inside a church. She couldn't even remember when the last time had been. She took everything in, taking a moment to just look at the pews full of women and children.

"Minx, over here," Alexis called, seeing her.

Alexis sat at a desk, transcribing the information being given to her by a petite Mexican woman cradling a small child.

With her hair pulled back in a neat ponytail and wearing a tracksuit, Alexis didn't look like the fabulous chick Minx had come to know. It was incredible how that girl could wear so many faces so convincingly. It was an art.

"I'll be finished in a second," Alexis promised, then turned back to the woman, speaking to her in fluent Spanish.

It took another ten minutes before the woman left.

Minx sat down.

"I didn't know you spoke Spanish."

Alexis shrugged. "My mother is Dominican."

Minx looked around.

"I haven't figured it out yet, but I know you *must* have an angle here."

"An angle? In a church for abused women? You really don't think much of me, do you?" Alexis replied.

"You just don't strike me as the volunteer type."

"I got caught shoplifting a few years ago. They sentenced me to community service and assigned me here. I liked it so much, I stayed. I come every Sunday," Alexis explained.

"So, this place is like your penitence for the bullshit you do?"

"I guess you could say that. All the dirt I do, I need to balance the scales a little. Build myself a few bricks in heaven."

Minx nodded.

"I guess I can respect that. But I need to talk to you. And not in here." She looked up at the ceiling.

Alexis understood, these weren't the words for under God's roof. She led Minx outside, to the back of the church.

"What's up?" Alexis inquired.

"We're going to rob the club."

"Wait, what? Rob what club? As in our club? Where we dance?"

"Are you fuckin' crazy? How? I mean..."

"Leave that to me. All I need to know is if you're down."

Alexis thought about it or a moment, and blew out her cheeks, shaking her head, but that was all it took. "I can't lie and say it hasn't crossed my mind as a score, but that fuckin' money room is fresh pussy tight. There's no way we're going to get in there, let alone get out again with that cash."

"Any door that locks can be unlocked," Minx said with a smirk. "Trust me, we're going to walk out of there and they won't know a thing."

"This I gotta hear."

"You're either in, or you're not," Minx warned her. "No backing out once I tell you what we're going to do. I'm serious, girl."

"I feel you. I'm in. Now tell me the how."

Minx explained the plan, and Alexis burst out laughing, like it was the funniest thing she'd heard in a long time. "God-damn, girl, that's ill! You a fuckin' genius."

"I know this, guy!" Minx fronted, doing a playful crip walk. She added, "But it's going to take three people. We need a third."

"Trust me, I know *just* the girl," Alexis assured her, then pulled out her phone and made a call.

COCO

Coco answered her phone on the second ring.

"Speak bitch," Coco greeted jokingly.

"I got something big for you," Alexis said.

"You know me girl, if it's over ten inches, I don't want it!"

"Nasty bitch, I ain't talkin' about dick. Where you at? I gotta tell you this face-to-face."

"Out of town. Let me hit you when I get back," Coco said.

"Say less."

Coco hung up and went back to putting on her ruby red lipstick. She took a deep breath, remembering Corey's words.

"This is going to make us a lot of money. Make this happen, and your name will ring bells with the boss."

The boss.

The mastermind.

The man Vita had sent her in to take down.

"You can do this girl," Coco told her reflection.

Deep down, she felt out of her depth. She'd run plenty of check and credit card scams, but running a straight con was different. This was much bigger. Thanks to her team though, she was now holding the keys to a 12-million-dollar mansion whose owner was on an overseas excursion, with a house-sitter had a cocaine addiction that was raging out of control.

"Please don't break anything," the young white girl had begged her, as she dropped the keys into Coco's palm and received the coke from Coco in return. She'd taken the dime bag greedily, desperate for it. If Coco had let her, she'd have snorted it off her tits, but Coco wanted the girl off the premises.

"You'll have the keys back before you know it," Coco promised.

And now she was minutes from pulling off the biggest scam of her life.

She watched the white couple pull up in their Maybach.

They were well into their sixties and reminded Coco of the Jetsons grown old and wrinkly.

"Let's make a movie," she mumbled to herself, as she put on her game face and stepped out of the car.

"Mrs. Crowell," the white woman called out, walking up to Coco, hand outstretched.

Coco shook it.

"Melody," she corrected her, with a lie, like they were old friends.

"Then I insist you call me Beverly."

"And I'm Lloyd," her husband chimed in, taking Coco's hand and kissing it, all Southern charm.

The look in his eyes left Coco in no doubt the old white man with a taste for chocolate, or at least liked the idea of trying it. She thought about it and realized that if it was the difference between pulling this off and not, she'd go through with it, though what that said about her she didn't want to know. She focused on the payout.

"Nice meeting you both. I hope the drive wasn't too arduous," Coco offered.

"Oh, not at all," Lloyd replied.

"Well then, if you're ready, your castle awaits," Coco said, giving them her commercial bright smile and showing them the way.

Once they were inside, Coco knew the house would sell itself.

Hell, she could've fallen for the scam herself if she had the money. It was something else.

"This place is beautiful," Beverly agreed, gushing over it before they'd done two rooms out of the many. "And I just *love* the décor. What an eye these people have. The furnishings are just perfect. I don't suppose the current owners would like to sell the house as is, contents and all?"

"We haven't discussed it, but I'm sure they would be amenable, just between us, they are kind of in a bind," Coco said, conspiratorially, drawing them into her confidence by lowering her voice a little as though worried about being overheard tattling secrets.

Lloyd's ear perked up. "Oh?"

Coco nodded. "I'm not supposed to be telling you this, given I'm representing *them*, but you guys seem like nice people who wouldn't take advantage of someone else's misfortune."

Coco knew the best way to scam is to make the mark think they're getting something over on you, or at least on the person you claim to be acting for.

Baited, Lloyd fell hook line and greedy sinker.

"I would never even think about it," he lied, obviously damn near salivating in his mind.

"Well, I've heard there's some kind of tax issue... seems like they may *have* to sell everything, even if they're selling cheap, just to pay it off. That's why they're having to let the house go in the first place."

Their greedy ears soaked it all up.

"How cheap?" Lloyd asked, betraying himself

"I'm not allowed to divulge their actual desired price," Coco replied. "I would if I could."

"Oh, come on, Melody. I can make it worth your while," Lloyd teased, pulling out his wallet and slipping her a few hundred dollars, like he thought she could be bought that cheaply.

Coco pushed it back. "No, I can't take that, I'm sorry. I will say this, but if you repeat it, I'll deny it."

"Our lips are sealed."

"Zip. In the vault."

"Well," Coco began, about to go for the kill, feeling her heartbeat increase at the thrill, knowing that she was so close. "If the IRS take possession, they've already got a sale lined up."

They both gasped.

"No."

"I'm afraid so."

"Well, okay, so what can we do to ensure that doesn't happen?" Lloyd wanted to know.

She blew out her cheeks. "If you can put down an option on the house today, I can finagle the paperwork to lock you in," Coco said. "They'll have no choice but to accept your legal claim."

Lloyd and Beverly looked at each other, their eyebrows raised, hunger racing.

"How much of an option?"

"A hundred thousand," Coco stated evenly.

"A hundred?" Lloyd guffawed.

"It's usually closer to ten cents on the dollar for the asking," she assured them.

"So, we're saying a million," Lloyd reasoned. "That's a steal for this place."

"A million one," Coco winked. "And yep, it's a steal."

Lloyd thought for a moment and then said, "Okay."

He pulled out his checkbook, ready to sign on the line.

"Ah, sorry. We can't take personal checks for an option. Options are only negotiable through bank certified checks," Coco explained.

Lloyd looked at Beverly.

"Well, I *could* run to the bank and have a cashier's check drawn up," Beverly offered.

"Melody, would it be too much of an inconvenience to you if we asked you to wait her a little while so we could take care of this?"

Coco looked at her watch as though pressed for time.

"Well..."

"I won't be long," Beverly assured her.

"Okay, but I do have another showing," Coco frowned. She knew that the woman was sold on the house, and she knew how much the old man wanted to please his lady. It didn't matter that she hadn't even seen the whole house. They were looking at the investment of a lifetime. A five-million-dollar crib for a fifth of the market value. It was too good to be true. There was no way they were going to miss out, even if they only bought it to flip.

"I'm on my way," Beverly said over her shoulder, as she hurried out the door.

As soon as the door closed, Lloyd turned to Coco with a leering smile.

"Mind showing me around the rest of the house?"

"Not at all," she said. "We've got time to kill."

Lloyd stayed a step behind Coco, watching her shapely ass wiggle to the rhythm of her strut.

By the time they got to the bedroom, Lloyd was done.

"I—umm—don't mean any disrespect so if I'm out of order, just let me know," he said, his confidence game not as solid when it came down to the crunch.

Coco could see the bulge in his pants so she already knew he was a goner.

"Yes?" she asked, the sweetness in her tone syrup-thick.

"If I offered you a thousand dollars—"

"I'd definitely be offended," Coco quickly cut him off.

"I'm sorry."

"But I like your watch."

It was a gold Rolex. He looked at it.

"My watch? This is a forty-thousand-dollar watch," he protested.

"And this is a forty-thousand-dollar ass," she reasoned, stepping closer to him. She ran her fingernails over his bulging crotch. "Don't you have insurance," she asked, suggesting a scam of his own to work.

He could report the watch stolen, get the pussy *and* his money back.

He liked the plan, proving that everyone's willing to become a con artist if they want something badly enough, and right then he wanted her.

Lloyd quickly took off the watch and dropped it in her hand.

By the time Beverly returned, Lloyd and Coco were downstairs, sitting on the couch, engaged in polite conversation like nothing that a forty-thousand dollar watch could buy had happened.

"I hope I didn't take too long," Beverly apologized, slightly out of breath.

She handed the check to Coco.

"No, you were right on time," Coco chuckled.

It was the easiest hundred grand she had ever made.

Devante cashed the check and gave her eighty grand of it.

She didn't begrudge him his cut, even at twenty large.

Too bad I can't keep it, she thought to herself, sourly.

But she had the Rolex, and no one needed to know anything about that little transaction.

She damn sure ain't getting her hands on it, she mumbled to herself. She took the money to Vita, signing the paperwork for the handover, then headed for the club to meet Alexis and Minx.

When they looped her in on what they were planning, she laughed. How could she not?

"Hell yeah, I'm with it, ladies," Coco cackled.

Not only would it be the opportunity for a big pay day, it offered a chance to get out from under Vita's thumb.

There was no way in hell she was going to tell the Fed about the plan.

ALEXIS

Alexis was always the center of attention wherever she went.

Industry parties were no different.

There were some bad bitches at KB's birthday party, and some basic ones, but she was definitely one of the baddest and she knew it.

She fit right in.

"Damn, baby, can I get you a drink?" One guy asked her, already drinking her in.

"Want to give me your number?" Asked another.

She wasn't biting.

"You ever been to Cancun, sweetness?" Said a third.

Offers of trips, cars, and jewelry came from every direction.

She suspected that some of the offers might even be genuine, but most of them were just bullshit; a line to get what they wanted and she wasn't falling for any of it, even though she was pretty sure she could come out ahead.

She had bigger fish to fry.

Alexis wasn't beat for conversation, but she already had her eyes on a major bag.

"What's up, birthday boy?" She greeted KB with a hug.

"You know how we do, ma. Since it's my birthday, you should be in your birthday suit," he joked, a leering grin on his face.

"Be careful what you wish for," Alexis whispered in his ear, reminding him what had happened the last time he'd tasted that fruit.

She was pretty sure that if his fiancée hadn't been at the party, he would've taken her up on the offer she hadn't actually made.

"Don't look now, but you see the dude Max Malone is talking to?" He said.

Alexis casually glanced around, side-eyeing who he was talking about. He was a slim guy in a smart suit, designer, well-cut. he looked like the kind of guy who had his hair trimmed every week.

"What about him?"

"He's fuckin' Max," KB replied.

"You got proof?"

"I will after tonight. I've got their room camera ready," he chuckled.

Alexis smiled.

He had really bought into the whole thing.

Max Malone was not only a major rapper, he'd just wrapped his first movie and the world was begging for him. She knew having Max on a leash would offer up access to the game's elite. It was hard to imagine *anyone* bigger at that moment in time.

"Good work," Alexis said.

He smiled and sipped his drink.

Too bad I'm no longer working for you, KB thought to himself.

As soon as he got Max on tape, he planned on giving it to both the new women in his life. Alexis and Vita. He had to admit, Alexis had a mean game, but double crossing her would make him the boss player.

Everyone's got a con, and he was going to enjoy bringing her down to size with his.

"Anything else?" Alexis probed.

"I'm working."

"Remember your quota," Alexis reminded him. "A deal's a deal."

"How could I forget?" He said sourly.

Alexis kissed him on the cheek.

"Happy birthday."

She made her way back through the crowd, checking her watch.

She was meant to hook up with Minx in less than an hour.

As much as she wanted to stay and work the room, she knew Minx wasn't the type of bitch you could just blow off.

She walked out of there, knowing that several sets of eyes were focused purely on her ass, but one pair was only concerned with her presence at the party for a very different reason.

It was Crow.

He had seen her come in and had been bulging with rage ever since.

Devante had told him how she had played him out of a half a million dollars, and that pissed had Crow off. Not because Devante was his man, but because the payoff was cutting into Crow's hustle.

Devante had been holding him down, breaking bread.

But once he had to pay off, he had to cut back on what he gave, so seeing her only served to remind him what she'd done.

But now he had a chance for payback.

Crow followed her out of the club.

There were too many people outside to make his move there and then, but he had already taken his first steps towards revenge.

Rule number one in the club, always carry your drink with your hand over it. Never walk through a crowd of people otherwise. But Alexis was too busy being cute to be safe, enjoying being the center of attention.

She hadn't even noticed he was there.

It was a slip-up she'd be very lucky if she lived to regret.

As she drove, the drug Crow had slipped into her drink began to take effect.

She grew drowsy, dangerously so.

The car drifted across the road.

The headlights blurred, the road tilted and Alexis's eyelids dropped.

Two wheels lost their grip. Tires dug into grass and the car began to slide until she was tilted down a bank.

The sudden shift of momentum startled her awake and sobered her for a moment, but it was too late to stop the car from hitting *something* and then the world was upside down.

If she hadn't been wearing her seatbelt, she'd have broken her neck.

Instead she got to walk away with a few bruises.

It was her lucky day.

She tried to get her bearings, lost, no idea what had happened or where she was.

Suddenly, her door flew open.

She looked at the face leaning in, sure it was a man, but struggling to focus. She didn't recognize Crow.

"Thank you," she muttered, thinking her savior was a good Samaritan.

"No, thank *you*, bitch," he said gruffly.

Her mind recognized his voice.

"Crow! No!"

Smack!

"Shut up!"

He released the seatbelt and dragged her out of the passenger seat.

"No, please! Somebody help!"

"Bitch, scream all you want. *Nobody* will hear you out here."

"Except me."

He heard the voice, but before he could turn around, he felt the blow on the back of his head that knocked him senseless. Blood ran down his face. He fell. Lying on his back, he looked up at Minx.

"What the—" he stammered, still seeing stars.

"Minx!"

The other woman glared at her.

"Stupid bitch! Why you say my *name*? Now, you have to kill the muthafuckah," Minx spat.

Alexis gasped.

"No, I can't!"

"Bitch, you better be glad I don't trust you," Minx remarked. "That was the only reason I was around to save your ass."

Minx held the tire iron out to Alexis.

"Take care of your business."

"I'm not a killer!" Alexis protested. "I can't do this."

"You leave him alive, he's coming back, sooner or later. And now he knows my name, he'll be after me, too," Minx warned. "You need to take care of this, and you need to do it now. Shit or get off the pot, girl."

Crow tried to get to his feet, but he was all arms and legs and none of them seemed to want to answer his brain.

"Please, I won't," he mumbled, the taste of his own blood in his mouth.

Alexis began to cry. She couldn't help herself.

"Don't make me do this."

Minx smiled a smile that chilled Alexis to the bone.

In that instant she knew exactly what the woman was capable of, and it went beyond the most chilling violence all the way to the heart of murder. Just like that.

"Fine, I'll do it. But once I finish with him, I'm gonna finish *you*."

Alexis knew she wasn't playing.

She looked at the tire iron in her hand.

She looked down at Crow.

"Alexis, I swear I won't bother you."

Too late for pleas.

Too late for anything.

She swung, hitting him in the face and breaking his nose.

The sound of the rupturing cartilage was sickening. But it also felt *good*. Alexis thought about the look on his face when he'd grabbed her and she swung again. This time she caught the side of his head.

He screamed out in pain.

"Shut him the fuck up," Minx ordered.

Alexis beat his face into jelly, losing herself in the violence. She frightened herself with just how much she enjoyed the brutal release.

Minx finally stopped her.

"He's dead. Time to go."

Alexis looked down at her handiwork. Crow's entire head had caved in and was now just a mass of blood, flesh and bone.

"Definitely closed casket," Minx chuckled, admiring her handiwork.

They dragged his body to Alexis's car, and pushed him inside, before they stuck a rag in the tank and set it all on fire.

In a moment it was a raging inferno.

Alexis couldn't take her eyes off it.

While killing the man had been easier than she had expected, watching the body burn was so much harder.

"We need to get out of here before it blows," Minx told her, grabbing her hand and pulling. "Report it stolen."

Minx drove Crow's car away. Alexis followed in Minx's car.

The woman owned her now.

Cool V wasn't the type of man to play with.

He ran a crew that had the game on lock.

David had already been to see him.

He'd thrown caution to the wind and made the pilgrimage to Cool V's sports bar, flashed his badge and thrown himself on the kingpin's mercy.

"Yeah. So? You're a cop. Should I be scared?" the bartender said, not even pausing as he polished a well-worn tumbler and put it back on the shelf.

David looked him in the eyes and replied, "Get V on the phone or I'm going to shoot you in the face and swear you went for a gun. Your call. Am I bluffing or am I that big of a cunt?"

The bartender blinked, but tried to keep a poker face.

"I ain't got one," he said, no sign of fear in his features, but it was there in his eyes.

"Don't worry, I've got one for you," David assured him. "I'm a regular boy scout. Prepared."

The bartender relented and got Cool V on the phone.

The man wasn't best pleased, but twenty minutes later, David was sitting across the table from Cool V in the back of the bar.

"So, you know where my wife is?" Cool V said. It was as much a statement as it was a question.

"I do."

"You fuckin' her?"

"I have."

"And you're telling me to show the green light... or else?"

"I am."

Cool V laughed in his face.

"You got a lot of nerve coming in here, Mr. Cop. That badge will only get you so far," Cool V warned.

"I know. I was counting on other things to ensure a little mutual cooperation between us from this day forward," David said, having a hand of his own to play.

Cool V smiled.

"Ah, I see. Like a marriage of inconvenience? You want to put in some work again?"

"No. I'll give you my territory," David said.

Cool V laughed.

"Your *territory*? Since when did you have any fucking *territory*. Motherfucka, you only eat because I let you eat. How you gonna bargain with borrowed chips?"

"Because I'm M.A.D."

"Huh?"

"M.A.D. Mutually Assured Destruction. You're a smart guy. You must have heard the term? It's what would happen if America and Russia ever really went to war. Nuclear. There'd be nothing left. We'd all die. No one wins, everybody loses," David gritted.

"And your point?"

"You might have the power of the street behind you, but I've got the biggest, bluest wall in America behind me. To take you down, I'd go down too, sure, I'm well aware of that, but it's a sacrifice I'd be willing to make to see her safe," David shrugged. It wasn't a threat. It was so much more than that. It was a beaten man pulling the pin.

Cool V looked him in the eyes for a moment before he spoke again. David wasn't going to be the first to blink; there was already far too much at stake.

"Are you telling me you'd *really* give up everything for that bitch? She ain't worth it."

"No need for insults," David said, putting his gun on the table. "Last thing either of us need is me pulling this trigger. You go, then your men send me after you. Mutually assured."

Cool V put his own gun on the table too.

"Then sue me." They were one surge of testosterone away from murdering each other. After a long stare, Cool V said, "Let me rephrase the question. Do you really think she's worth it? Do you even really know who she is?"

David wanted to lie, but his hesitation gave him away.

"The accident... blurred her memory," David admitted. "She doesn't really know herself."

Cool V laughed in his face.

"So, you have no idea what she's capable of, huh? Interesting. And pretty funny from where I'm sitting." Cool V paused, a smile playing across his lips. "Okay, lover boy. You think you know my wife? You don't know shit."

"Either you're going to tell me, or you ain't, and I figure you like to talk, am I right?"

"Oh, I'm going to tell you. Then, you can tell me if you still want to tear this city down over a piece of pussy..."

"Cover the church! The gunfire is coming from the church!" Sergeant Maxwell screamed over the furious staccato rat-tat-tat *of automatic gunfire.*

Haiti was a living hell.

The heat, the poverty, the killings, the blood. But he'd been sent to do a job and that's what he intended to do. He'd been a marine for three years before his team had been sent to hell, one mission: take down a drug kingpin for the US government. A little unofficial interference.

"I'm going in," he yelled, sprinting across the open yard in front of the church, exposing himself to enemy gunfire. His team covered him, pinning the enemy down.

Through the doors, he saw the bodies of several Haitian gunmen.

But they weren't all he saw...

Dozens of naked women and girls; several of them were dead, but not all of them.

"*Cease fire!*" *He screamed.*

They had no intel on women in the church. Nothing had come back to them about the place was being used to traffic women.

"*Damn,*" *he mumbled, feeling a surge of grief and guilt in the face of the dead women. He couldn't save them.*

He walked amongst the dead, finding the body of the Haitian drug kingpin, and beneath him, the most beautiful woman he had ever seen. It was hard seeing beauty in all of this ugliness. Maxwell pulled the man's body off her, and hated himself for looking at her nakedness. Even among the carnage, she was a goddess.

"*Do you speak English?*" *He asked.*

She nodded.

He found a priest's robe and gave it to her.

"*Put this on,*" *he told her.*

"*He-he was going to kill us. You saved us,*" *she sobbed. She had a Creole-tinged accent.*

His team rounded the survivors up and took them back to the base. Most were from other Caribbean countries, all of them attractive. He refused to let the goddess out of his sight.

"*What's your name?*" *he asked.*

"*Jordan,*" *she replied timidly.*

When he returned to America, he arranged to take her with him. But that wasn't all he was able to take back.

Maxwell took the Haitian kingpin's entire distribution network with him. Once his tour was over, he wasted no time locking shit down. He went from being Sergeant Victor Maxwell, just another soldier like so many others, to Cool V someone with serious clout, and his name rang bells.

His love affair with Jordan blossomed, and within six months, they were married and inseparable.

"Or so I thought," Cool V spat disgustedly. He had finished telling his tale. It was ancient history. He took a breath and then downed his drink.

"What do you mean by that?"

"She started acting... strangely. She would wake up in the middle of the night in cold sweats, mumbling shit in Creole. I didn't know what the hell was going on. More than once, she swore someone was in the room with us. I tried to sooth her, but I can't be there 24/7 to slay her bogeymen. I was too busy in the streets. I guess that's when Spaz got inside her head and did his damage..."

"V sent me to check on you," Spaz said, as soon as Jordan opened the door.

She knew right away that was a lie.

But she didn't care.

Ever since she had first laid eyes on Spaz, she knew he was the one. She'd been with V largely out of a sense of gratitude, he'd saved her, the problem was he felt more than that. He had been her savior after all, and had the complex that went along with it.

She owed him.

He owned her.

"Come in," she invited, stepping aside to allow Spaz inside.

As he passed, he breathed deeply, taking in the scent of her White Diamond perfume. She shut the door and turned to him. She was wearing a silk robe that clung to her body.

"So, why didn't he come himself?" She asked.

Spaz shrugged. "He was busy, I guess."

"He's always busy."

"You have to pay the price of being the boss. That's the way it goes."

"I don't need a boss; I need a husband. I need someone who's here, not somewhere else all most of the time. I need—"

"Seems to me you need a friend even more," Spaz said.

She looked at him.

"Do you have someone in mind?"

"Why not me?"

She smirked, folding her arms over her breasts, fully aware that he'd barely taken his eyes off them since she'd let him in. Hell, she craved that attention as much as he wanted to give it to her.

"And what would Victor say if he heard you say that?"

"We both know that doesn't matter to you. Come on, I've seen the way you look at me. The glances. The side-eye. You've been calling my name since we first met."

"This is true, but what about the way you look at me?"

Spaz stepped closer.

"Like you're real tasty, and I'm a hungry man."

"How hungry?"

"Starving."

"Then I guess you'd better show me."

Weeks passed before she finally confided in him, offering the secret she'd been too afraid to share until she knew she had him. "Victor beats me."

Spaz wanted to kill him, but he wanted something else more.

"We could run away," he suggested.

"And go where?"

"Anywhere, as long as we're together, I don't care."

"What will we do for money?" she asked.

And so, the plan was born.

"She took a suitcase full of money when she left," Cool V told David, leading the sorry story to its natural conclusion.

"She doesn't have it anymore," David said. "At least I haven't seen it."

Cool V shrugged.

"Maybe the police recovered it in the accident."

David knew that wasn't the case. "Maybe the bang on the head just means that she can't remember where it is?"

V snorted, clearly unimpressed with the idea. "You want her?" he said after a moment. "I've got a simple business proposal for you: find my money and you can have her."

Later, David thought of all this as he brought Jordan to orgasm.

"What's wrong, baby? Are you okay?" She asked, contented but exhausted.

David sat up on the side of the bed.

"I went to see Victor," he told her.

She seized his arm, suddenly alert, and with panic in her eyes. The fear there was palpable.

"Why? What if he had you followed? He'll find me!"

"I'm a cop. He knows what will happen if he does," David told her.

"He's killed cops before," Jordan said. "You know he has. He wouldn't hesitate to do it again."

David didn't respond to that. Instead, he said, "Where's the money, Jordan?"

"What money?"

He looked at her coldly.

"Please don't play with me. Victor told me everything. He

told me about Haiti, about Spaz and the affair, and about the money you took."

"And you *believed* him?"

"Why would he lie to me? Face-to-face. He had nothing to gain, and haven't told me shit. It is what it is. He's not going to leave us be until he gets it back. So, I'll ask you again, where is it? We turn it over to him, we get our lives back."

"I don't know. I don't remember any money."

"Okay, say I believe you. How do you know it's not true?" He knew he was going down a dangerous road, but there was no way they were going to get past this unless he knew the truth about what had happened and she was her only avenue to that truth.

"Look around, David. I live in a run-down boarding house. I strip for a living. If I stole his money, why would I live like *this*? Don't you think I'd be living somewhere *better*?"

"I don't know. You tell me? Maybe this is all part of the scam?" David said. "But, I'll be honest with you, Jordan, I don't think Victor has made this all up. There *has* to be some truth in it somewhere along the line."

Jordan thought about Minx and the counterfeit money she had stashed under the bed. *Minx. That girl has to be the key. What does she know about this?* Jordan asked herself. *Was that the missing money? And if it was how the fuck had she got hold of it?*

David didn't know what to believe.

Everything Victor had said made sense, but Jordan was right. Why did he want her dead so bad? Was it really just about money? He could stand losing a few grand. Was it just face?

"I told you, my life is complicated," Jordan said eventually.

"Tell me about *Les Nubians*."

Hearing the name of the singers instantly sparked a memory in Jordan's head that brought a smile to her face. It flickered and faded fast.

She was in Haiti, laughing. The moon was full. *Les Nubians* were singing their remake of Sade's "Sweetest Taboo" in French. Jordan was dressed in an all-white outfit and then, just like that, the memory was gone.

"I remember them. I don't know why."

"He said they were your favorite," David said.

Jordan buried her face in her hands.

"I don't know what to do. What to say... I don't *know* anything."

David moved her hands to uncover her face.

"He said, if you give back the money, he'd let you live, and we need never hear from him again. If you've got it, or know where it is, just tell me, I'll take care of it. We can be free of this." "I swear, I don't know anything about any money."

"It's in there," he said, "We just have to find a way to dislodge it in your mind," David said. "Problem is, I don't have a clue how we do that."

"What if he's lying?"

David looked her in the eyes. "What if he's not?"

Jordan nodded. He was right. She had to find out the truth. If there was any stolen money in her past, what had she done with it?

She knew just who to ask.

———

"And you believed Minx knew something about the money?" Myers asked, moving up to the witness box. This was it. Moving towards the confession that would damn her.

"Yes, yes I did."

"And did you confront her?"

"I did."

"What happened?" Myers pressed, leaning forward, suddenly feeling more interested in what she might have to say.

Jordan took a deep breath and replied, "I killed her."

COCO

"Damn, I hate asking this bitch for a goddamn thing," Coco mumbled as she approached Alexis in the dressing room, but she felt like she had no other choice.

Vita was monopolizing her time, as well as skimming the money she earned for evidence. It was a catch-22 all right. She had her federal stipend that came in the mail every week, but that was barely enough to pay her rent, and the cash she got from selling the last mark's watch was long gone.

It turned out the damned thing had a serial number and that meant it could be traced so she'd had to pawn it for a fraction of its worth to a dealer who'd ask no questions. She was pretty sure the guy intended to keep it for himself.

She was desperate and she knew there was one well that never ran dry.

Hey girl!" Coco gushed with fake love, as she embraced Alexis.

"You already know, bitch. Chasing that bag," Alexis sang, dancing silly and provocatively at the same time.

"Shit, that's exactly what I need to talk to you about."

"What's up, boo?"

"A bitch needs a hook up. My bills are due and my life ain't poppin'," Coco complained.

Alexis took Coco's hand and they both sat down.

"Girl, you should've hollered as soon as you knew things weren't good. You *know* I got you, right? What you need?"

"Remember how you did it for me before with that credit move? When I gave you my social security number? You gave me ten grand. Well, whatever you did, I need you to make that move again," Coco said. "Or some kinda magic that shakes the money tree. I'm dying here."

Alexis sat back and acted as though she was contemplating the move when in truth, she was one hundred percent going to move on it. Truth be told, she'd long been eating off Coco's social without her knowing. Alexis knew she owed Coco, but she wasn't about to tell her that.

"I tell you what. I'll do it, but I can't do ten grand," Alexis said, twisting her lips.

Here goes this bitch with her bullshit, Coco thought, but said, "So what *can* you do?"

"7500. Maybe."

"Seventy-five? Maybe? Come on, bitch. This is me! We s'posed to be girls."

"We are, but damn, shit's tight," Alexis lied. "Ain't no good if we get busted."

Coco shook her head. She knew she had to take it, but that didn't mean she had to *like* it.

"When?"

"Tomorrow after five. But I'll need your social again," Alexis lied. She already knew it by heart.

Coco wrote it down and passed her the slip of paper.

"Don't spin me, Lex," Coco pouted.

"Don't worry, I got you."

They fake hugged with about as much warmth as penguins trapped in an ice floe.

"When are we supposed to rob the club?" Coco asked.

"Shhh! Damn, bitch, you want the *world* to know? I ain't told Minx you're in yet."

"Well, tell her. Let's get it poppin', damn."

Coco was thirsty. She needed money and was ready to do whatever it took to get it. Her phone rang. It was Flacco.

"What's up?" she answered.

"Where you at?" he asked.

"Around," Coco replied, giving nothing away.

"Well, you need to get down here. I got someone who wants to meet you."

Coco sighed.

"How much he spendin', Flacco? 'Cause for real—"

"Naw. It's bigger than that. It's him," Flacco half-whispered. "Him."

She knew exactly who Flacco was talking about.

The mastermind, the person she was supposed to be helping to bring down.

"Meet me?"

"He says he likes how you move. He has something big for you."

Coco's heart leapt in her chest.

This could be her big break.

The question was, should she share it with Vita?

If Vita found out she'd met the mastermind and hadn't reported it, Coco was sure the fed would send her to jail, no questions, do not pass go, do not collect her C.I. stipend. *But* if she met him, *and* he put her on a major come-up, she could disappear.

And that was what she wanted to.

"You still there?" Flacco asked when she didn't say anything for a moment.

"Yeah. Where should I go?"

"That little café on Market Street."

He hung up.

Coco tucked her cellphone away.

"I'll see you tomorrow," Coco said to Minx. "Gotta go."

"Say less."

As she drove, Coco contemplated her dilemma with Vita.

She decided to see the mastermind first, and find out what he had in mind for her. It wasn't worth reporting back if the job he wanted her to do wasn't properly big. A quick flip, she could bail cash in hand. Anything else, she'd tell Vita she was onto the big man. At least that way there wouldn't be any blow back.

She pulled up to the café, parked, then waited.

Ten minutes later, Flacco called.

"A blue Prius is going to pull up. When it does, get in."

He hung up.

True to his word, a few moments later, the blue Prius pulled up alongside her, facing in the opposite direction. The young white girl driving rolled down her window. She didn't give a crap that she was holding up traffic.

"Leave your phone in the car," she told Coco.

Coco reached over and put her phone in the glove compartment, making sure the white girl registered the move.

She hoped she wasn't about to make the biggest mistake of her life.

She got out of the car and walked around to get in the Prius.

The girl didn't say another word.

The silent ride took her out of the city to a small quiet suburb, through its identical soulless streets, before eventually they arrived at a small house.

"Come on," the white girl beckoned her gruffly.

Under normal circumstances, that would've made Coco smack the shit out of her, but Coco was way too nervous to recognize the attitude let alone do anything about it. She felt like Dorothy finally meeting the Wizard.

Together, they walked in the house.

"He's in the basement," the white girl told her and pointed her in the right direction.

Coco headed down the stairs.

She was on edge.

No idea what waited for her down there.

The basement was plush and fully furnished. What she didn't know was that it was also soundproof and insulated against listening devices. For some reason, she'd expected to see a white man, instead she saw a black man. A fine ass Black man.

"Come in," he gruffed, deep bass. "Welcome."

"Haven't I seen you somewhere before?" she asked. She was pretty sure she'd seen his face somewhere, but couldn't place it. It was another thing lost in her missing memory.

"I guess I just have a common face because, trust me, if I'd met you before I would've kept you close," he eyed her with an obvious appreciation for her beauty.

"It's good to meet you. I appreciate this opportunity."

"How do you know you'll want the job?" He asked, reasonably.

"Because I want the money," she said honestly.

"So, you're willing to do anything for a bag?"

"Depends on how big the bag is," Coco shrugged, again the truth. Always better to run a con with as much truth behind it as possible.

He chuckled. "I like a bitch with no bottom. A man can go deep."

"If he's man enough," she replied.

"Point taken. So, you ready to get down to business?"

"Definitely," she said.

"Then strip."

Coco looked at him with one eyebrow raised, but paused for no more than a heartbeat.

"Straight to the point, aren't we?"

"I need to be sure you're not wearing a wire."

"I'm not a cop."

"Then you have nothing to hide," he said.

Coco kicked off her heels then wiggled out of her skirt to reveal a mauve-colored thong. She then slipped off her blouse to show that she was wearing nothing underneath, not even a bra.

"Satisfied?" she sassed.

He sipped his drink without taking his eyes off her, enjoying the view.

"Not quite," he said. "Turn around."

She turned and gave him a full view of one of the most beautiful asses he'd ever seen.

He stepped over and picked up her clothes, carefully going through them. She looked at him.

"I feel like I should squat, spread 'em and cough," Coco quipped.

"Just a precaution, ma. Can't ever been too careful in this

business," he said. The smile on his face suddenly reminded her of a shark. She felt a cold shiver run up a spine. It was a warning she was prepared to ignore, for now.

His eyes caressed her figure, giving her goosebumps.

He tossed her clothes onto a small couch.

"Can I get dressed now?"

"No," he smiled, adding, "It's not every day a man gets the chance to behold such a masterpiece. Drink?" he offered.

"Henny and coke," she replied, settling into the comfort of her own nudity.

"The ancients used to believe that a woman's naked beauty was the most powerful muse," he told her, after he'd poured two out.

He handed her the drink.

"So, you brought me all the way out here for a naked history lesson?"

"No, but I like the way you get to the point. Actually, you are the point. I'm going to put you in charge of fifty women. Your own team. You'll be in charge of check scams, credit card scams and a little identity theft. Your cut will be ten percent of everything," he said. "If you think you're up to it?"

Coco couldn't believe her ears.

Her mind lighting up like the Vegas slots flashing up 'jackpot!' until she remembered Vita.

There was no way she could go in that deep and keep it from her.

Which meant she was going to have to let her know.

Which meant no payout. All of that money, none of it for her.

"You don't look happy," he said, pulling her out of her thoughts.

"No, no, I am. It's just... Why me?"

He smiled.

"I've been watching you for a while. I like the way you move. You know how to make the game work for you. So, what do you say?"

"I say, hell yeah."

"I thought you might."

"So, when do I start?"

"I'll introduce you to your connects in a few days. You've already got about twenty chicks under you. The rest you'll have to recruit yourself," he explained.

"That ain't no problem," she assured him.

"Just make sure you choose wisely. One bad apple..."

"Can I get my clothes now?"

He put his drink down, slid down his zipper, and pulled out his already-erect nine inches.

"Not until I introduce you to a friend of mine," he said. "If you get my money like you got this dick, we both gonna be rich."

Coco couldn't wait.

———

"He wants you to do *what*?" Vita could barely conceal her excitement; this was it, pay dirt. It was everything she'd been waiting for, without ever being sure that it would come.

"He's putting me in charge of a fuckin' team of female scammers," Coco repeated, laying it out in the simplest of terms.

As soon as she left the mastermind's crib, she set up a meeting with Vita; there was no point in putting it off. Coco knew what he was asking for was going to lead to a big pay off, but not an immediate one. So, she figured her best bet was to bring Vita in and hope to buy enough time for the club robbery, so she could disappear like a thief in the night before it all went sideways.

She thought she had it all figured out.

"Do you know what this could mean? This fuckin' case can make my career. I'm talking about the Rico Act and a promotion," Vita said.

"What about me?" Coco asked.

Vita stopped and looked at her.

"You make this case for me, you bring me his team on a platter, and this is what I'll do for you. I'll let you walk. And if you have cash in your pocket from it, I'll look the other way. Just don't get caught lifting it."

Coco's eyes bulged, not quite believing what she was hearing. "All the money?"

"Every dime. You'll have to turn enough of it in to be tagged as evidence, but once the case is closed, evidence has a habit of disappearing," Vita said.

"Wait. You can do that?" Coco couldn't quite believe what she was hearing. There was an old saying about the sniff test, if something smelled like shit it probably was shit. But what if? The woman had seemed straight as a die and yet here she was promising a pay-off.

Vita shrugged. "It happens all the time. What do you think happens to the money we confiscate? It gets spent as 'buy money,' in undercover operations, things like that. But plenty slips through the cracks sooner or later."

"Even the feds have a scam." Coco's greed went to 100. She started to think about how much money might be involved. If she could keep the money she made off fifty scammers... those were numbers she couldn't run in her head. "Don't worry, I'll make it happen," she promised, and she meant every word.

MINX

S he followed the woman, stealthy as a cat, never letting her concentration lapse. She had zero intention of being noticed. Minx had an eye for anomalies, and she knew exactly when something didn't fit. It was hard-coded into her DNA.

Minx had been coming out of the club when she'd spotted Alexis talking to the small Spanish woman.

She recognized the woman from the church women's shelter.

Her instincts kicked in there and then. She knew *exactly* what was going on, but to satisfy her own measure of doubt, she knew she needed to follow the woman.

The Spanish woman was on foot, so Minx left her car in the parking lot and walked behind her, keeping a safe distance.

The woman didn't turn around once, no doubt not even considering herself interesting enough to follow.

Minx tracked her to a large house on the edge of the city.

Only then, climbing the stoop, did the Spanish woman

look around, and even then it was barely more than a quick glance before she hurried up the few short stairs to the door.

Minx hid in the shadow of one of the trees that lined the street, watching the Spanish woman disappear inside.

What are you into, Alexis? Minx wondered, as she crept through the darkness, moving right up to the house. She ghosted along the front, trying to get a look in through the windows. The curtains were all closed. She heard the murmur of voices through the glass. Many voices. Too many of them. Something inside Minx burned; instincts sensed the reality of the situation, but she still needed to *see* for herself. Seeing was believing.

She stealthed her way up to the back door and quietly picked the lock. It took her all of twelve seconds before she heard the satisfying *click* of it opening. She turned the knob and entered.

The smell of too many females in one place hit her as she moved deeper into the house.

The sounds of sex filled the air. Ugly sounds. Not seductions. No sweet nothings. This was bought and paid for grunting and ownership.

Everywhere she looked, she caught glimpses of bodies. It was an orgy of bare flesh.

She'd walked on into a hoe house.

Minx recognized some of the women from the shelter.

Now she understood Alexis's angle and why she was volunteering at the church. She was prostituting these poor bitches.

"Goddamn, princess, I ain't never seen *you* here before," a butt-naked fat dude grunted, waddling up to Minx, his dick swinging. "How much?"

Minx didn't hesitate.

"Your life," she rasped, spitting the razor from her mouth, and slitting his throat in one smooth motion.

She was glad she'd thought to put it in place.

It happened so fast no one even noticed, and it was too dark to see the arc of the arterial spray.

Some of it landed on a couple fucking doggy style a few feet away, hot blood, but they didn't seem to notice—or care.

Minx turned the dying man face down on the rug and held his spasming body down.

"Just relax, ugly. It's almost over," she whispered in his ear.

He twitched once more then lay still.

Minx melted out of the room, lingering just long enough to lock the image of the broken shelter women into her mind.

Now I don't need to feel guilty about what I'm gonna do to you, Alexis, because it's gonna be far worse, Minx thought as she crept back out the door.

COCO

Coco knew just how to build her team.

She hit up the strip clubs, the hair salons, and the chicks in line at the county jail, because they were the most desperate. It didn't take long to recruit eighteen potential new team members, and raw as they were, every one of them fit what she was looking for: young and hungry.

"Pay attention and learn how it's done," she explained.

They watched and listened, hanging on her every word like she was college prof teaching Check Scamming 101.

"It's all about the look. Most tellers are women; white women, most of the time. They make a judgement call about the customer on the other side of the glass without even thinking about it. So, if you come in with a blue dress, tattoos everywhere, popping gum with a five-thousand-dollar check, it's going to set off all sorts of subconscious warning signs," Coco explained.

"That's some racist bullshit," remarked one gum-popping thot.

"Naw, it's just good business. It's all in the presentation. So, invest in a wig; black, straight, and long. Cover those tattoos with make-up, lose the gum, smile, and be polite. Use good words, no ghetto slang, no small talk. Nothing that might give you away. You stick to the rules and you'll make money," she said. "Ignore them and I can guarantee that you won't. More to the point, you'll find yourself in front of a judge, and I'm not going to be able to save you. 'Coz I ain't got no sway with the bench. You feel me?"

And make money they did and plenty of it.

By the end of the week, she had 33 girls hitting up every bank in the city and had already moved into the territories beyond, the smaller branches and the Credit Unions. The money was stacking up.

Coco was on top of the world.

And all the girls working for her had money in their pockets, more than most of them had ever held before.

"Don't worry, I'm keeping track of every dime," Vita remarked when Coco met her, offering the low down on the latest scam. She handed over her slice of the action.

"You don't need to worry. This is going to be big. Believe me. This is just the start of it."

Coco knew she was definitely on the up.

She drove along the highway, feeling like her future was as bright as the beautiful summer day she was savoring.

She pulled into her condo's parking lot and slid her car into her usual space. It was all routine. And routines got you killed. She was gripped by the sense that something wasn't right. Nothing looked out of place, but it just felt *off* somehow.

Several pairs of blue jeans skidded up towards her from all directions, and all of them aimed guns at her face.

"Get out of the car!"

"Don't move!"

"Get down on the ground!"

Conflicting commands were thrown at her, and there was zero chance she could obey all of them, meaning some dumb fuck was bound to pull the trigger. She tried to figure out what was going down. Her fingers trembled over the ignition key, tempted to restart the engine, but that was suicide. All those guns? No chance she'd get out of there without getting capped.

"Federal agents."

When she heard the words, she felt a degree of relief that washed over her. She threw up her hands and yelled back, "It's okay! I'm with you!"

The agents rushed the car and snatched her out of the driver's seat. They bundled her to the ground and cuffed her tight.

"Why are you doing this? I told you, I'm with *you*," she repeated, as they stuffed her into the backseat of one of their vehicles.

They didn't care who she was with; that much was obvious.

They drove her to the federal building in the heart of the city, entering via an underground parking lot, and frog-marched her to a private elevator, which rose in gravity defying silence to the 18th floor.

Once they had her in the interrogation room, and cuffed to the table two white male agents came in, starting in on the interrogation.

"I'm Agent Johnson and this is Agent Kramer," Johnson, who looked like a poor copy of that actor with a particular skill set, said. He dropped into a chair on the other side of the table.

"Do you know why you're here?" Kramer asked.

"I haven't got a fucking clue. There's got to be some sort of mistake. I—"

"There's no mistake, Ms. Hopkins," Kramer cut her off sharply. "You are a polygamous woman taken to the extreme."

Coco's eyes got big.

"A poly-what?"

Johnson cut in smoothly. "A polygamist. You're married to at least 25 men; interestingly they are all foreigners, from Nigeria, China, Russia, Mexico, and Honduras. And I'm willing to guess this might just be the tip of the iceberg."

Coco shook her head.

"I ain't married to nobody."

Johnson put a thick folder on the table and opened it up.

There looked like a hell of a lot of paper in there.

"Really? These are signed marriage certificates. Would you care to look at them and confirm whose name and social security number are on them?"

She looked. Sure enough, she saw her name, but it was when she saw the signature, it all came together in a sting. It wasn't hers, but she would know that handwriting anywhere.

Alexis.

She'd been using Coco's name and social security number to marry her to men who wanted citizenship. That was the scam. Every time Alexis had given her cash it had come from the money she'd made marrying her off to foreigners.

"That dirty fuckin' bitch," Coco said, shaking her head. She wanted to laugh, but the last thing it was was funny.

"Can you explain this?" Kramer questioned.

"I sure can. See, that's my name, sure, and that's my Social, but that's not *my* signature."

"No?"

"No. But I know whose it is."

"Who?"

Coco shook her head. Not that easy. "Look, I know what

this looks like, but looks ain't worth shit. I work for you. I'm telling you. I work for the feds."

Johnson and Kramer looked at one another, then back at her.

"How exactly do you work for us?" Kramer echoed, with a hint of a smirk.

"Call Agent Vita Lewis. She'll straighten this out," Coco told them.

"Agent Lewis?" Johnson repeated.

"Yes."

"And she's an agent in *this* field office?"

"I don't know what a field office is, but she has an office on the other end of Market Street," Coco explained.

Johnson sat back, clearly taken.

"Okay, you lost me. She has an office that isn't in this federal building?"

Coco's heart began to sink.

"She said she was undercover so she had a separate..." Coco's voice trailed off as she started to feel her whole world suddenly closing in on her in the heartbeat before it began to fall apart around her ears.

She shook her head.

It couldn't be true, she thought to herself.

Kramer couldn't hold back any longer. He leaned his head back and roared with laughter. "And you fell for *that*?" Kramer cackled like it was the funniest thing he'd ever heard.

Coco felt completely played.

"So... you mean she's not a federal agent?" Coco said, desperately clutching at straws.

"I'm afraid not," Johnson said.

Coco couldn't believe her ears.

"But she had the federal symbol in her office..." she stammered, realizing how foolish she must have sounded. A fucking symbol and a fucking flag. Basic. She'd been tricked. Vita had fucking used her and taken all her money. She'd been setting people up, but the whole time she had been the one getting set up.

Everybody gets scammed.

"What does this woman look like?" Kramer questioned.

"Black, middle-aged woman. Auntie chubby."

Kramer slid a picture across the table for her.

"Does she look like this, perhaps?"

Coco looked at the picture and gasped.

"Hell yeah! That's the lyin' bitch right there," she spat. "That's the woman who called herself Agent Lewis. Who the fuck is she really?"

Johnson nodded.

"Her name isn't Lewis. It's Denise Blackman. She's a county clerk. She's the person who signed all of these marriage licenses."

"A county clerk?"

"Whenever someone gets married, the license must be signed by a clerk. What appears to have happened is Denise Blackman partnered with someone—"

"Alexis. Alexis Pratt," Coco dropped the bitch's name. There was no stopping her. She would tell them everything she knew about the pair of them. They'd fucked her over and she wasn't going to hold back. This wasn't being an informant, it wasn't snitching, it was fucking payback.

Kramer nodded, non-committedly, "—with this Alexis Pratt and agreed to certify these fraudulent licenses for money."

"They played the shit out of me," Coco admitted.

"Where is Blackman now?" Kramer asked.

"I could give her up right now. But," she was thinking on her feet, trying to find an angle to shovel her way clear of this shit. "What if I could give you everybody? All in one go?"

"What do you mean by everybody?" Johnson probed, interested.

"Alexis, Vita, or Blackman or whatever the fuck she's really called, all at once with a robbery to boot."

"A robbery? Do you mean a bank robbery?" Johnson asked.

Coco shook her head.

"A club robbery."

"That's not our jurisdiction," Kramer remarked dismissively.

"It is when I tell you who's really running the whole show," Coco teased. She'd buried the lead.

Kramer and Johnson looked at each other, then back at her.

Johnson said, "Keep talking."

JORDAN

"You lied to us."

"Us? I—" David stammered. The gun in his face made him realize jut how unstable she really was.

Minx kept the gun at eye-level, just out of his reach.

In the time it would have taken him to close the gap she would have been able to pull the trigger. And they both knew it. The best thing he could do was to keep her calm. No accidental trigger pulls.

"You knew the whole fuckin' time," she said.

"No. That's not true. Yes, I know, but only since I went to see Victor," he admitted.

Minx cocked the hammer.

"I want to know everything," she demanded. "And you're gonna tell me. No being economical with the truth."

"Okay, I'll tell you. But put the gun down."

"Who the hell are you?" she growled.

David took a deep breath and began...

DAVID'S STORY

In a million years, he never thought he'd become a crooked cop.

He never even imagined he'd be a cop at all.

Or that his name would be David.

"Michael, didn't I tell you to go to the store?" His mother yelled from the kitchen.

"Yes ma'am," he yelled back.

He was fifteen and living with his mother in Miami.

She was a pretty woman. A bank teller. She loved her son with all her heart, but she kept making bad choices when it came to men. It had started before his father, and it hadn't ended with him.

He went to the corner store to get his mother a quart of milk.

It was a trip that would change his life.

He returned to the sound of loud, angry voices and he recognized both of them despite the anger. His whole body tensed up as he walked into the living room.

"Bitch, don't *lie* to me! I know you fucked him!"

He heard the accusation coming from the back room, his mother's bedroom. The one place in the house he was no longer allowed to go into when she wasn't alone.

"Steve, I told you I—"

Smack!

Michael ran straight into the room to find Steve choking his mother.

"Get the fuck off my mother," he screamed, trying to pry the guy's hands off her, but he was much bigger than Michael, and so much stronger. There wasn't a lot her could do, but that didn't mean he wasn't going to try it all; he'd never forgive himself if he didn't.

Steve back-handed him so hard that he flew off the bed and landed hard on his back, knocking the breath out of him.

"You little *motherfuckah*, I'll teach you to interfere in grown-up folks' business," Steve rasped, pulling out a Rambo knife.

"Michael," his mother screamed as Steve grabbed him by the throat, his face rage-red, blood vessels on the verge of bursting. Spittle flew from his mouth.

Steve looked like he was ready to gut him.

Her ribs were broken and her eyes swollen almost shut, but seeing her son in danger gave his mom a boost of maternal energy, like a she-lion protecting her cub.

She shrieked as she jumped on Steve's back, clawing at his eyes, and bit his ear damned near in half. She clung on as if his life depended on it. And maybe it did.

"Bitch," Steve howled, relinquishing his hold on the boy.

He swung the knife straight back into her chest without a moment's thought.

"Mama!" Michael bellowed, feeling every burning inch of the blade going in.

She looked at Michael, the light of life going out of her.

The knife had gone straight through her heart.

It was a sight he would never forget.

Steve drew the knife out, smeared with blood, and turned to him. "You're next, you fuckin' little faggot."

Michael knew he couldn't beat Steve, not now, not with his bare hands up against that murdering bastard's knife, but he vowed that one day he would even the score.

He took off running, younger, faster, fitter, and lost Steve in the steamy Miami night.

Michael was heartbroken. He had nowhere to go, and no other family. For days that turned into weeks and weeks that wound their way into months, he wandered Miami, eating out of garbage bins and soup kitchens and surviving off the kindness of strangers.

By the time he was sixteen, he was a hardened kid of the street.

"Hey you, kid! Get the fuck outta my fuckin' dumpster!" the grizzly bum yelled, hobbling along the alley towards him.

Michael was knee-deep in the dumpster, rummaging for anything to eat. This particular dumpster was behind a newly opened Dunkin Donuts. By the rules of the street, new restaurants were open season for the first few weeks, then the garbage became the property of whoever was strong enough to claim it. But the bum saw Michael's small wiry frame and wanted more than just garbage; he wanted Michael too.

"This ain't your dumpster," Michael retorted, as the bum started to climb inside.

"Boy, you want to eat, you pay around here, and I ain't talkin' about money," the bum spat, grabbing his crotch. Michael knew how it was. He'd seen men and women raped and assaulted for scraps of food. It was a case of survival of the fittest, and he was determined to survive.

169

"This is a free zone. I can take what I want," Michael said, voice hard. Show no fear.

"Ain't shit free, boy, and I'm gonna teach you that," the bum spat, then with an agility that belied his size, caught Michael with a vicious right hook that knocked him flat on his ass, sprawling in trash. Before Michael could get up, the bum was on his chest, choking the life out of him.

"Make it easy on yourself, boy, and I'll let you live... as my bitch!" the bum cackled, like he was Jay Leno.

Michael felt himself starting to lose his grip on consciousness, a blackness creeping in at the edges of his vision. He knew once he passed out, the bum would do whatever he wanted, and maybe he wouldn't wake up at all. That thought gave him the strength to dig around the garbage until he felt a bottle. He closed his fingers around it, gripping it tight, and swung with everything he had.

The bottle caught the bum square on the temple, dazing him.

A second blow knocked him off balance.

The bum grunted, and toppled to the side, hitting his head on the dumpster with a sickening thump.

With adrenaline and fear firing through his veins, Michael didn't give the bum a chance to recover. He fell on top of the bum and began wailing on him with the bottle until it finally broke, then stabbed him in the neck with the busted glass again and again, until he was too exhausted to continue.

The bum was long dead, but Michael had been snared in a bloodlust he couldn't snap out of.

When he finally ran out of steam, he saw what he had done.

It was his first kill.

It wouldn't be his last.

I've got to get out of here, his mind told him.

He hopped out of the dumpster and ran as fast he could, as far away from the bloody corpse of the bum as he could. At least no one would miss the bum or report him missing. It gave him a chance to run. But what he was really running away from was the feeling; the elation he had got from taking a life. And that would follow him wherever he went.

Now, as he sat huddled in the bushes in a dark park, he knew who his next kill must be. He headed back to the side of Miami where Steve was from. He knew where he lived; he'd been there with his mother a number of times. It was a small, single story, brick home he shared with his grandmother.

Michael crept up on the house, listening carefully as he approached. He peeked in through the living room window and saw Steve's grandmother in an armchair, nodding in front of the evening news like she was approving all of the sins and woes of the world one after the other.

He headed around to the back of the house.

He peered in through window after window until he saw Steve in his bedroom. He wasn't alone. Some young girl was giving him head.

Michael tried the window, but it was locked.

He went around another circuit of the downstairs until he found the window of the master bedroom, cracked wide enough to give him his point of entry. He climbed in through the window and slunk low to the floor, waiting as he listened for any movement. Nothing. He rose to his full height and stepped slowly out of the room, slipping past the grandmother into the kitchen where he went through the knife draw to select the biggest blade he could find before headed through to Steve's bedroom.

The girl moaned.

Michael watched from the door.

Steve's back was to him.

He was too busy to hear his executioner's approach.

"For my momma," Michael spat, then rammed the blade into Steve's neck. The knife went so deep it stuck, wedging into muscle and bone. Steve staggered away, screaming, his hard-on failing him as the blood gouted out of his neck.

"Get it out!"

The young girl screamed at the sight of the dying man and the crazed killer. She tried to run out, but Michael wasn't about to let her ruin the moment. He punched her so hard she went down, one punch and out.

Steve sank to his knees, a look of surprise on his face as he looked up into the eyes of the little runt he'd promised to kill not so long ago.

"I-I'm gonna kill you," Steve stammered.

Michael eyed a bat in the corner and walked slowly across the room to heft it, slapping the meat of it off his palm.

"You're already dead," Michael said, then stood over Steve and began to beat him to death one vicious swing at a time before he could bleed out.

When he was finished, Michael turned to see the grandmother walking in with a .38 snub pointed at him.

"Drop the bat," she said, her voice firm despite her frailty.

"He killed my mother," Michael answered, looking her in the eyes.

"You want to go join her? Drop the bat," she repeated, cocking the hammer.

Michael let the bat fall from his hand.

"The police are on their way," she said.

"Then you might as well kill me, 'cause I ain't going to prison," he replied, with determination.

She looked at him evenly.

"You say my grandson killed your mama?"

Michael nodded.

"That girl over in Liberty City, huh?"

"Yes."

She nodded.

"I seen that on the news. Remembered her face coming over here. Yours too. She seemed nice enough."

"She was my momma. She wasn't nice. She was my world. I'm leaving. If you gonna shoot, shoot," Michael told her, then slowly backed his way to the window.

She didn't lower the gun, but he knew she wouldn't shoot him.

He climbed out of the window and never saw her again. After that, he knew he had to get out of Miami. But where could he go ?

His question was solved when he came across a man selling false identities. It was then that Michael Foster died, never to be heard from again, and David Wingate was born.

He needed to give this new identity a history, so he joined the military.

David felt that if his new identity were a military man, people would be less inclined to question it. If anything, he might even get *more* respect. Besides, where else could he legally quench his thirst for blood? It didn't take him long to distinguish himself in the field. He did two tours in Afghanistan, slaying Taliban and questionable civilians without second thought. In his eyes they were all enemy combatants. He became proficient with a rifle, but he was better in hand-to-hand combat, close quarters, knives gnashing like teeth. That was when his bloodlust raged and he found real satisfaction.

He was honorably discharged from the army, and like so many other veterans, became a police officer.

The job continued to support his fake identity.

The academy accepted him without question, and once he was a cop, no one questioned him. He felt safe. Until his bloodlust betrayed him.

Answering a domestic dispute call with his partner, they arrived at the scene as the man beat on his unconscious wife. The moment took him back to his mother and Steve.

"Don't fucking move!" his partner shouted, ordering the man at gunpoint.

He stopped and raised his bloodied hands.

He looked up at both David and his partner, both guns trained on him.

"Whatever you say, officers," he smirked. "You got me. This... just a little disagreement. You know what women be like, they get under your skin, nag, nag, nag, chipping away. It's enough to drive you out of your mind."

"Step away from the woman," David growled.

The man complied, but there was zero remorse or contrition.

The guy laughed.

It was the laugh that did it.

David felt like the man was taunting them. He was just like Steve, an arrogant piece of shit woman-beater, and in that moment, it was as though the ghost of Steve's grinning face was superimposed on top of this one. He didn't deserve to live.

Boc!

The first shot surprised both the man and David's partner, Teddy. It sounded impossibly loud in the small room.

"You shot me! You motherfucker, you shot me!" The man howled, grimacing as the blood bloomed on his shirt. The message hadn't quite reached his brain, until he slumped to the floor.

"Officer Wingate!" Teddy barked. "What the *fuck*?"

"He moved for a weapon," David seethed. "You saw it."

The man lay writhing in pain.

"I didn't do anything. You fuckin' shot me!"

David stood over him, gun aimed at his face.

When the man saw the dead look in David's eyes, he froze, his expression changing from surprise to panic.

"Apologize," David spat.

"Officer Wingate!"

"I'm sorry," the man yelled. "I'm sorry, okay? I swear. I'm sorry. I swear to the Virgin Mary and all that's fuckin' holy, I'm sorry."

"You repent, now you can die in peace," David said, coldly. "You might even get into your heaven if you believe hard enough."

"Please don't kill me! Please!" The man sobbed.

"You see that? That's what it feels like to live in fear," David hissed, adding, "And this is how it feels to die, hoping it ends."

"Dav—"

Boc! Boc! Boc!

David pumped three bullets into the man, one in his hip, another in his shoulder, but the third hit him straight in his heart. He varied the shots on purpose; something he'd learned in the army. It would make it look more like a struggle.

The woman was still unconscious.

Teddy looked at David.

"What the fuck was that all about?" His partner looked at him like something had broken.

"Justice," David responded.

Teddy shook his head.

"You shouldn't have killed him."

"Why didn't you stop me?"

"Maybe I was scared you'd shoot me, too," Teddy said, and maybe he was. But David doubted it.

The humor defused the tension.

The story was the man struggled, he went for a gun. A gun Teddy provided from his ankle holster.

"Where did you get that?" David asked.

"Ask me no questions, I'll tell you no lies," Teddy fronted.

Teddy had David's back, but only because he had his own agenda. Teddy was dirty. A few days later they pulled over two young gang-bangers and their girlfriends, and it was time for David to have his back.

"Where's it at?" Teddy demanded.

Nobody said anything.

"Oh? Nobody knows nothing? I'll tell you what..."

Teddy snatched one of the girls out of the car.

"Hey!"

"Shut the fuck up," Teddy barked, bending her over the trunk of the car.

Her phat juicy ass peeked out from under her short skirt. David winced, but he remained silent, knowing that there was nothing he could say that would make a difference. Meanwhile, Teddy dug in her pussy.

"You perverted motherfucka," she spat.

But Teddy wasn't trying to get his freak on, he knew how these gang-bangers got down.

"Put it in the bitch's pussy."

Sure enough...

"Bingo!" he cackled, holding up the Ziploc full of opioids.

The girl sobbed.

Teddy smelled the bag.

"Damn bitch, you need to douche. Now, I'm going to ask you again. Where's it at? If I don't get answers this time, I'm taking all of you to jail."

By the time it was over, he had $800 worth of pills.

He put them right back on the streets and money in his pocket.

"I don't know, Teddy. Drugs?" David said, uncomfortable with his involvement and looking the other way. His thing, he'd taken a fucking wife-beater off the streets... this hurt ordinary kids. Teddy didn't see things the same way.

"It's no worse than murder," he shrugged, giving David a subtle reminder.

That's how it really started.

Before he knew it, the two of them were bringing in five grand a week from a nice little side hustle of drugs. Teddy called it recycling, always laughing at his own jokes. It was going smoothly until Teddy came to him one day and said, "Bro, I got a guy that wants to meet you."

That guy turned out to be Cool V.

They met in the back of V's restaurant. His man Spaz escorted them to V's office. Everyone shook hands. It was cordial. Businesslike. With no more introduction than that, Cool V got down to it.

"I want you to work for me."

"Not interested," David replied.

He wasn't sure that he liked the look of the guy and he had no need for any more than he was already getting. Greed, contrary to the old movie, wasn't good. Greed got you killed.

"Hold up, Dave, let's hear the man out," Teddy reasoned.

"Look, we've got our own thing going on. No offense intended, but we don't need another hand to feed," David said.

"It's not about you feeding me. Your partner says you're

handy with a firearm," Cool V stated. It wasn't a question. And like his piece, it was loaded.

"Okay," David replied cautiously, not happy that his partner had been so free talking about him behind his back.

"I'm thinking we have a coincidence of wants and needs is all. You take care of a few jobs for me, I'll make sure I throw a few busts your way to help you both make detectives and everyone's happy."

David shook his head.

"Not interested."

Cool V chuckled.

"Come on, brah. I'm *sure* we can work something out... Michael."

Hearing the name he had left behind was like the feel of cold steel pressed hard to his temple; a revelation that could blow the brains out of the identity he had taken.

Teddy looked confused. "Who's Michael?"

"Why don't you ask your partner?" Cool V said, enjoying the fact he knew something the bent cop didn't. "I'm sure he'll fill you in."

David glared at him. He thought about pulling his gun and killing the man on the spot, but V read his mind.

"You'll never make it out of the building," Cool V warned. "Hell, you won't even make it out of this room."

The tension grew thick.

Nothing was said for several moments while Cool V and David stared, each willing the other to blink first, like rutting stags ready to lock horns.

"You're wondering how I know, but that's the wrong question. You need to ask yourself who else might know. But don't worry, your secret's safe with me as long as we have an understanding," Cool V smirked.

"How did you find out?"

He knew he'd been careful, but wanted to know where and how he'd slipped up.

"It wasn't hard. Anybody who really digs can find it. But I can make it real untraceable. That's my offer. In exchange, you do five hits for me. You do that, we're even."

"Five? Who do hate that much?" He was only slightly surprised that he was considering going along with it.

"It's not about hate, and we'll get to the names once I know where you stand," Cool V said his voice calm and even.

A beat.

"Five?"

"Five."

Another beat.

"Okay," David said. "Fine. And you make Michael disappear again?"

"As good as gone already."

And so David became a hitman with a badge.

Then, it was a natural slide into V's other businesses. He became a credit card scammer, eventually running a team of chicks that put him on top. He rose and rose, becoming the mastermind to V's kingpin. He was the man Flacco worked for, the man Coco worked for.

But he wasn't free.

He still owed Cool V one more hit.

"Spaz? Your man?" David asked.

Cool V nodded.

"He's planning on trying to take something very valuable from me," Cool V replied.

"So why not kill him yourself?"

"I have my reasons. All you need to know is this hit clears us. Number five. After this, you're free," Cool V reminded him.

David nodded. "Then Spaz it is."

The night Spaz and Jordan made their escape, it had been David who chased them down, driving up beside the bike to shoot Spaz in the face. The machine had slid under him when David hit him with the second shot. Dead men can't drive a machine. Unbalanced, the weight of his corpse sent the bike sliding across the road and into the path on any oncoming truck.

Somehow the woman on the back had been thrown clear.

He hadn't known it was Jordan.

He never knew that the stripper he'd meet was Jordan.

He never knew he'd fall in love.

"You're lying! You knew!" Minx raved. "You must have known."

"It would be easy to think so, but I didn't."

"I've heard enough."

"I love you!" David screamed at the other woman in the room.

Boc! Boc! Two shots in the chest.

"David!" Jordan's scream was visceral. His body slumped to the floor, one hand moving toward his chest but falling limp long before it reached his heart.

"What have you done?" Jordan cried, falling at his side. She didn't know what to do. To think. Minx was talking. She couldn't focus on the words.

"I had to. He was going to fuck everything up!"

"I love him... loved... fuck."

"More than me?"

"I *hate* you!"

"You don't mean that."

Jordan glared. "I've never meant anything more in my life."

Minx bristled. "So, what are you saying?"

"It's over. I'm done. You're dead to me."

"You're not in charge. I am."

"Bitch, you heard what I said."

"You leave, it'll be in a body bag," Minx threatened.

Jordan lunged.

They clashed like two hell cats full of fists and fury.

"I'm gonna kill you," Minx swore.

Jordan didn't waste words. She slung Minx against the wall. They slammed each other all over the room, battering seven shades of shit out of each other until Jordan finally got the upper hand. She rolled on top of Minx, pinning her. Her hand took a grip on her throat, nails digging in deep either side of her trachea, and began to choke the life out of her as Minx clawed at her face and then, desperately, at her hands.

"Get off me," she screamed, thrashing about in an attempt to throw Jordan off her, but she wasn't about to be bucked.

"Die, you fucking bitch, just die," Jordan raged, increasing the pressure, putting her every ounce of strength she had into it, nails sinking so deep they drew blood, and determined not to give up no matter what the other woman did.

Minx's fight lost its vigor, her eyes slowly lost their glow.

She looked up at Jordan.

Her eyes said, *why?* but she'd never know the answer.

The last breath left her body.

Exhausted, Jordan rolled away and lay on her back, breathing heavily. She'd won, though what had she won really? Her life? She'd never thought of herself as a fighter, and never a match for that crazy ass bitch, but she'd proved something to herself. A dark something. Her thoughts instantly turned to the money that she knew was hers by right.

It might be counterfeit, but she knew the plan and that made it as good as real.

She crawled over to David, his body lifeless, and kissed his cheek. "I'm so sorry, baby. I do love you," she sniffled, and left him for the rats that would eventually come crawling out of the walls.

Jordan retrieved the suitcase full of money from where it had been stashed under the bed, and had been about to leave when David's phone rang. She should have left it. Let it ring off into the messages. She didn't. She grabbed it and checked the screen.

She saw the caller's name.

It was Coco.

It didn't make was. What the hell was Coco doing calling David?

Something wasn't right.

She waited until it stopped ringing, then texted: *Can't talk. What's up?*

She waited, then Coco texted back: *I got the money.*

Her curiosity piqued, Jorden wrote: *Cool. Will hit you in a minute.*

She was definitely going to get to the bottom of this.

COCO

"He didn't answer," Coco informed Agent Johnson. "He's just texted to say he can't talk."

"Text him back," he suggested.

Coco did as she was told.

"He said he'll hit me in a minute," Coco reported after a brief exchange of texts. She was surprised he hadn't insisted on watching what she was typing.

Johnson sat back and nodded.

"If everything works out, and this dirty cop really is the scam mastermind, you'll walk. You have my word. But if you're bullshitting us, you fry, and neither of us will shed a tear."

"Trust me, he is," she assured him.

Just because she knew he was, that wasn't going to be enough to save her. She was going to have to *prove* it to them. She had no qualms about handing the lot of them over to the authorities if it was going to save her neck. That was the rule of this particular jungle.

Her phone rang.

It was Jordan.

Without waiting to get the nod from Agent Johnson, she answered.

"What's up, bitch?" Coco greeted, trying to sound nonchalant.

Johnson couldn't hear Jordan's side of the conversation, so when Coco hung up, he asked, "What was that all about?"

"The robbery. It's going down. She wants to see me."

"You're wearing a wire," he demanded.

Reluctantly, she nodded. It wasn't as though she had a choice.

ALEXIS

*C*all *me ASAP.*

Alexis saw the text from Minx, then tucked her phone into her purse. She was pretty sure she knew what it was about, but she had bigger fish on the hook.

Max Malone.

Minx had already told her to make sure she had the biggest ballers coming to the club on the night of the robbery. She wanted pervert's row filled with Ballers and Trick's while the girls chummed the waters. They way, the club was assured of having plenty of money on hand. The more, the better.

Max Malone might have thought he was on top of the world, but Alexis knew who was on top of *him*, and that was what counted. She intended to use that knowledge to her advantage.

Alexis rose in the glass elevator as swiftly and as gracefully as bubbles in a champagne flute, arriving at the hotel's penthouse floor in a matter of seconds. She stepped out and knocked on the door of Max Malone's suite. It opened smoothly a second later.

He'd been waiting.

"You must be Alexis," Max said, smiling as he stepped aside to allow her to into the suite.

Stepping inside, Alexis assessed him as he shut the door, then took a moment to apply the same scrutiny to the room. It appeared to be empty, but she knew they weren't alone.

"Thank you for the meeting," she said.

Max kissed her hand.

"Any friend of KB's is a friend of mine," he said. "Drink?"

"No. I'd rather get down to business, if that's ok with you?"

He raised an eyebrow. She tried not to smile at that moment, even though the poor sap didn't have a clue of what was about to hit him.

"Business?"

She held out her phone and pressed play.

He saw himself being fucked from behind by a muscular white dude. From the shrieks and cries he had loved every minute of it. Good for him. There was no mistaking the anger in his eyes now, though. He'd seen enough.

"Where the hell did you get that?"

"KB," she snickered. "Some friend, huh?"

"How much?" Max seethed.

"Three."

"Three million? You've got to be out of your fuckin' mind, ma."

"Three souls. Let me explain. This isn't about you. It's about something more. Don't get me wrong, you will pay, but not in dollars, in favors. When I say jump, you say—"

"How fuckin' high?" he growled.

The line might have become a cliché, but that didn't stop it feeling good.

"Exactly. But, in the meantime, you'll give me three more

moneymakers with secrets they'd rather not become public. At the same time, you'll also have this on them. Now, of course you can't *use* it, not without my approval, but they won't know that, will they? Get the picture?"

Max nodded.

"I do. So, you want me to blackmail three people, people with reputations they give a shit about, for you?"

"Yep. You got a problem with that?"

"Nope. And I do this, you won't hang me out to dry?"

"And kill my golden goose? Of course not," she said, at least as not for as long as it serve her purpose. "You have my word."

Max smiled.

"Then I guess we've got a deal."

They shook hands, a little reluctantly on Max's part, bargain struck with the devil. Alexis headed for the door.

"Oh, and I also if you're looking to earn some brownie points, bring all your famous friends to my club on Saturday night. There's going to be a special show, so you won't want to be late. Trust me."

As soon as she got into the elevator and hit the button to descend, she called Minx.

"I've got Malone."

VITA

She had no idea she was being followed, but Vita knew something wasn't right.

It was a sixth sense thing.

She had been in the game long enough to know that her gut instinct was rarely wrong. And right then, that second, it was screaming, "Run!"

Unfortunately, her greed was shouting equally loudly and she never had been able to ignore the score.

She'd come up with the idea of impersonating a federal agent after watching a documentary about a crew that called themselves the Wild Cowboys back in the '80s. They'd impersonate police officers, complete with uniforms and badges, raid stash houses and confiscate the drugs and money. It was a short-lived game, but it paid dividends well out of proportion with the risk while it lasted.

She wanted something more long-term.

She wanted something that would build, not just lead to a fast buck and burn out.

As a county clerk, she had access to all manner of official documents, state seals, and things that together would sell her façade. The biggest trick was the office with the federal seal. When people walked in and saw it up on the wall, that seal was a wrap. They believed every word, no matter what she told them.

She'd cleaned up to the tune of over a million dollars from fooling people into selling drugs, running credit card scams, and on occasion even prostitution rings, all while the mark thought they were confidential informants working for the feds and therefore above the law.

It was a good scam.

So good she'd even started to think of them as her C.I.s.

But this was the biggest lick she had ever hit.

She had Coco, and Coco had at least fifty scammers working under her, all bringing in close to five grand a day. Vita knew, at that rate, she'd make over five million in a year. That kind of return was paydirt. Gold rush. Bonanza. The whales were making it rain.

Little did she know, her days were numbered.

Her phone rang.

"Yeah?"

"I've got Malone," Alexis said.

Vita smiled.

"So, the club is going to be packed," Vita said. "Good girl."

"Just like we want it. Remember, be ready and we walk away with everything," Alexis said, as if either of them needed reminding what was at stake here. They had everything to play for, and everything was a score beyond the extent of most folks imaginings, but not hers.

"How could I forget?"

They laughed, a we're in this together moment of intimacy, then hung up. Everything was in place down to the last detail, and she couldn't wait.

THE ROBBERY

The stage was set. Literally. Jordan danced on it, drawing every eye in her direction, while Alexis and Coco worked the room.

And what a room it was.

It was packed with some of the biggest ballers, there were proper A list names, and gangstas sitting side by side them, filling out perverts row and the tables beyond it. The feds were there, too. Agents Johnson and Kramer. Coco had explained everything to them. They were watching the whales while the girls chummed the waters, waiting for it all to go down. Coco had been specific. There was only one way this played out right, so they were gonna have to trust her if they wanted to haul the lot of them off to county and bask in the publicity of this huge bust. And both of those boys had their own ambitions. They wanted to be special agents.

Everybody has a scam of their own.

You ready? Alexis texted Vita.

Born ready, Vita's text came back.

From her side, Alexis wanted the robbery to go down so

Vita could act like a Fed and 'arrest' both Coco and Jordan. Then the pair of them could walk out the front door with the money, no one any the wiser.

It was a solid plan.

But for the fact that Vita was planning on killing all three. *Fuck a fake badge when you can use a real bullet*, she thought. It was all coming together so well; everything was falling into place. She could almost taste the dead presidents on her tongue, and they smelled pussy sweet.

Jordan worked the pole while the ballers made it rain dollars. The beat pulsed. The lights strobed. Other girls worked the rows, offering air dances, or ground it out on laps that belonged to the kings of this city.

When her set was through, she gathered up her paper and sauntered over to join Coco and Alexis in the shadows while another girl took her place as eye bait.

"Y'all ready?"

"You know it," Coco sang.

"Let's do this," Alexis said.

They headed through to the locker room. There were three other strippers in there, getting ready for their turns up front. At first, they paid Jordan no attention, but that changed once the girls had put on the dread wigs and the sleek all-black mechanic jumpsuits. One girl side-eyed them, asking," What the fuck y'all bitches got going on?"

Jordan walked up to where she sat, leaned in and stuck the muzzle of a Desert Eagle up hard to her forehead and answered, "Do you *really* wanna to know?"

The girl shook her head, beads of sweat breaking out at her temple.

"Tie these bitches up," Jordan ordered. "We don't want

them squealing before we're out of here. After that it'll be too late."

They bound two of them up with plastic ties and the other with a pair of bondage cuffs they found in a drawer. Once they were secured, Jordan cocked her pistol and loosed a primal scream. "Let's go get rich!"

———

Myers shook his head and stepped away from the witness stand.

He breathed out, more of a sigh than a judgement, fascinated by the way this story of hers was playing out before the jury.

He turned back to Jordan in the witness box. He looked from her to the judge and back to her. He waited for her to explain, but when she didn't he asked, "This was Minx's plan, right?"

"Yes, it was," she admitted.

"And you expect us to believe that you killed her and took over?"

Jordan held her head up, met his gaze, held it. Eye to eye.

"I'm simply telling the story. You believe what you will. I swore to tell no lies."

"No, you're telling us half the story! I don't believe you killed Minx."

"I did."

"No, you didn't. You know why I know?" Myers leered.

"Why?"

"Because I believe I'm talking to Minx right now."

That jury of her peers gasped, a ripple of surprise and confusion spreading through the twelve of them.

Jordan's lawyer was on his feet and shouting his objections before the hush descended again. "We've already established the defendant has been suffering with dissociative identity disorder, your honor, a split personality brought on by severe head trauma as a result of the accident."

Before the judge could sustain or overrule, Myers cut in. "No, your honor, the defense's *theory* is that Ms. Kincaid is suffering from this dissociative identity, we've seen no evidence of that any personality spilt. Far from it, in fact. I believe she is the notorious Minx from the Haitian mafia," Myers said.

Jordan cried, tracks of silent tears wet on her cheeks. "I'm —I'm just a girl from Georgia," she said.

"Interesting you should say that, because when we checked births, deaths and marriages, as well as full social security and background checks, no we found that out of a population of 9.68 million people, not a single Jordan Kincaid exists in Georgia. So, why don't you tell us who you really are?" Myers grilled.

"Would you please let her finish the story," her lawyer requested reluctantly. Myers nodded. Jordan wiped her tears and continued.

"Everybody hit the ground. Now!" Jordan bellowed through her ski mask, brandishing the pistol in the air.

Brrr-brrr-brappp!

Alexis held her finger on the trigger and let her automatic AK-47 rip, filling the ceiling with lead to show it wasn't a game.

The whole club ate the carpet as the ceiling tiles showered them with falling plaster.

196

"Let's move!" Coco screamed.

They pushed the manager back to the money room.

"Open it!" Jordan demanded.

He did, trembling but co-operative. If he recognized their voices, he didn't let on. He twisted the rotary dial on the safe, back and forth to the dance of the combination only he knew.

Inside stacks of bills sat big and pretty, just waiting for them to be picked up and taken away.

"Let's get it," Alexis cackled, beginning to load the money into the black trash bags Jordan gave them.

Back in the main dancefloor, Coco kept an eye on the crowd while Kramer and Johnson kept an eye on her.

Every few seconds she glanced back towards the money room.

It was taking too long.

Someone out here was gonna become a hero.

And die in the process.

There were too many egos trapped in the room.

There was always going to be one stupid enough to fuck everything up for her.

"Don't even think about it," she told every last one of them.

She could see them twitching. Itching.

In the money room, bags filled, Jordan hollered, "Every-body scatter!"

Boc! Boc!

Alexis and Coco were caught off guard, but it gave Jordan a chance to switch the garbage filled with money with the garbage bags she'd stuffed with the counterfeit bills.

She did it so smoothly, no one suspected a thing. She was absolutely sure of it. Sweet as honey, and twice as slick.

"Let's go!" Jordan barked.

They shot out the back door, snatching off their masks and

stripping out of their jumpsuits so that they could blend effortlessly with the crowd. After all, everyone expected them to be there. They were the entertainment they'd been staring at all night.

"Freeze!" Vita yelled as they came bursting out of the club.

"No, *you* freeze!" another voice screamed at her. Agent Kramer, his gun trained on Vita.

Vita didn't hesitate.

Boc! Boc!

She aimed for Kramer, but he was already moving. She missed.

But so did he.

Boc!

His second shot split her forehead, killing her instantly.

Jordan looked down at the woman's dead body and knew that it was over.

"So, you think because the money was counterfeit, you're going to side-step any sort of punishment?" Myers chuckled. "A woman is dead, and there are a trail of bodies leading up to her."

He didn't know about the switch, she realized. She resisted the temptation to smile.

"I'm innocent," Jordan repeated the plea she'd given when she set foot on the stand.

"I would suggest that's for a jury to decide, not for you to tell us," he said, content that his cross had crucified her.

And decide they did. Six hours later.

The jury foreman rose to his feet as the judge asked if they had a verdict. "We do, your honor. In the case of the United

States vs Jordan Kinkaid we find the defendant not guilty, your honor."

The courtroom erupted.

Jordan had won. She couldn't believe it. Nor could half the people in the courtroom, who stacked the prosecution benches.

"Thank you for all you've done," she said to her lawyer, pressing her hand into his.

She looked at the D.A. and smiled.

"It's not over," Myers hissed.

"No, it's not," she confessed and the dead-eye coldness in her gaze sent a shiver up his spine.

Jordan entered the underground parking lot. She had won. It was clean. Done. Double jeopardy meant she wasn't getting hauled back to answer for the same crimes again, whatever name they tried her under. And not a single one of them suspected the switch.

The money was at the club where she had stashed it.

All she had to do was go back and fetch it.

Click!

She heard the gun cock.

She turned around.

And faced a ghost.

"I don't... David... you're dead..."

He smirked, keeping the black eye of his gun trained on her.

"That's what you wanted, you treacherous bitch. You didn't even check to see if I was still breathing. You left me to die," he spat. "You didn't even think that I might have been wearing a vest. I knew you were crazy, but I didn't know you were Minx!"

Now she'd won, there was no need to maintain the charade.

She smiled.

"I can be whoever I want to be," she said. "Jordan, the good girl, I like her, but Minx fits me so much better though, don't you think?"

"Not as much as a casket," Cool V said as he stepped out from behind one of the parked cars behind her.

Minx shook her head, like she couldn't quite believe the extend of this ghost's betrayal.

"David, I thought you loved me? You gave me up?"

"I thought you loved me until you shot me! The love kinda dried up after that," he said flatly.

"Where's my money, bitch?" Cool V demanded, crossing the hardstand to get right up into her face.

"You're going to kill me anyway. So, fuck you," Minx hissed.

Cool V shrugged.

"Well, there's your fifth kill, Michael. Don't miss this time."

"Michael?" Minx echoed.

David chuckled.

"Looks like you weren't the only one running a scam, Minx."

He wanted to shoot but he couldn't bring himself to do it.

In that moment he realized that despite it all, he actually loved her.

That was unexpected. He hadn't thought himself the sentimental type. Not since Steve had shown him what that twisted version of love was worth.

Love complicated things.

But lead had a way of making them simple.

He turned the gun on Cool V.

"Number five, I'm free."

Boc!

The shot opened up a red blossom in the middle of Cool V's forehead but exploded out the back of his skull.

"I didn't... I thought you'd kill me. After I... but didn't. You saved me? Why" Minx said.

David tucked the gun in his waist and crossed the few steps between them to wrap his arms around her.

"I guess when it came right down to it, I bought your scam so hard I fell in love too much to kill you."

She kissed him then, nothing but the truth in the moment for the first time in all the hours they'd shared together.

"I love you, too," she said so quietly he could barely hear the words, even with her lips pressed up to his ear.

Boc!

"But I love me more," she told his corpse as she released her hold on him, and his dead feet stumbled back, dancing as his legs betrayed him.

She'd shot him with his own gun.

But once wasn't enough.

She'd made that mistake before.

She aimed at his face.

"No vest on your face," she said, ending it once and for all.

Boc!

Blood spattered everywhere. She laughed. Her enemies were gone. There was no one left to stop her.

She'd won.

All she had to do was drive back to the club and pick up the money. She didn't know where she was going to go next, but she couldn't stay here. Nature abhors a vacuum. There would be people rising up to looking to take Cool V's place.

She had no intention of getting snared up in the middle of *that*.

She still had people she had leverage over, there were plenty of people out there who owed her, but she could do that from anywhere, and be anyone she wanted to be.

THE END

THANK YOU

We truly hope you enjoyed this title from Kingston Imperial. Our company prides itself on breaking new authors, as well as working with established ones to create incredible reading content to amplify your literary experience. In an effort to keep our movement going, we urge all readers to leave a review (hopefully positive) and let us know what you think. This will not only spread the word to more readers, but it will allow us the opportunity to continue providing you with more titles to read. Thank you for being a part of our journey and for writing a review.

KINGSTON IMPERIAL

Marvis Johnson — Publisher
Kathy Iandoli — Editorial Director
Joshua Wirth — Designer
Bob Newman — Publicist

Contact:
Kingston Imperial
144 North 7th Street #255
Brooklyn, NY 11249
Email: Info@kingstonimperial.com
www.kingstonimperial.com

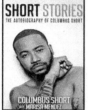

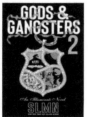

CPSIA information can be obtained
at www.ICGtesting.com
Printed in the USA
LVHW050323030321
680360LV00004B/4